Ponciá Vicencio

Conceição Evaristo

Ponciá Vicencio

Conceição Evaristo

translated from the Portugese by
Paloma Martinez-Cruz

HOST PUBLICATIONS
AUSTIN, TX

Host Publications, Inc. 1000 East 7th, Suite 201, Austin, TX 78702

Layout and Design: Joe Bratcher & Anand Ramaswamy
Cover Art: Jaime Vargas
Cover Design: Anand Ramaswamy

Library of Congress Catalog Number: 2006934722
ISBN 10: 0-924047-33-X (hardcover)
ISBN 10: 0-924047-34-8 (softcover)

ISBN 13: 978-0-924047-33-6 (hardcover)
ISBN 13: 978-0-924047-34-3 (softcover)

First Edition

Introduction

Appearing in 2003 in Portuguese, it is a great privilege to present Conceição Evaristo's *Ponciá Vicencio* in English here for the first time. "I had become accustomed to saying," writes Maria José Somerlate Barbosa in the original preface, "that Conceição Evaristo's poetry is deeply visceral, profoundly marked by hidden words meticulously chosen for their verbal and emotional impact on readers. After reading *Ponciá Vicencio*, I found that many similarities exist between her poetry and her narrative…Many times the subtlety of what is not pronounced or explained…is precisely what brings richness to the text." In creating the character Ponciá Vicencio, a woman contending with the multiple oppressions presented by the categories of race, class and gender, Evaristo's spare language tells the story of survival that, despite centuries of censorship in the forms of lash, noose and severe economic privation, emerges here as a unique celebration of Afro-Brazilian womanhood.

As both a powerful literary achievement and a black Atlantic liberatory project, the novel illuminates aspects of urban and rural Latin American conditions with poetic eloquence and raw urgency. As Evaristo's heroine Ponciá Vicencio pieces together the fragments of her family's past, she manages not only to unearth the root causes of their community's suffering, but also to embrace the survival of African mysteries in the Americas. Her characters collaborate with a hemispheric African-American spirituality that neither claims African purity nor American originality, but rather joins the two in a voice that is entirely Brazilian.

Conceição Evaristo was born in Belo Horizonte in the state of Minas Gerais. In an interview published in 2002, Evaristo tells Elzbieta Szoka "I was born in a large slum in Belo Horizonte, and

I grew up in it. I grew up listening to my family telling stories of slavery." The consolidation of a uniquely Afro-Brazilian identity politics began to emerge as a significant force in the 1980's, marked in the world of literary expression by the formation of a literary journal called *Quilombhoje*. Evaristo's writings answer this groups' call to reinvision Brazil's national narratives in their own image.

Because Evaristo's creative language is as invested in transforming individual and social consciousness as it is in artistic innovation, it is fitting to strive for the greatest possible inclusion here rather than to risk silencing the Afro-Brazilian transmissions of meaning that are central to her story. My present remarks attempt to provide some context for Brazilian terms and allusions that may not be as immediate to Western readers as to their Brazilian counterparts. I organize my explanations of these terms and references in order of their appearance in the novel, which leaves the novel's pages unburdened by the interference of footnotes and elaborations. I conclude with a reflection on the language problems that we confront when seemingly uncomplicated Brazilian Portuguese prose is translated into United States English.

The novel opens onto Ponciá who, as an adult, feels a shudder of fright as she contemplates a rainbow, recalling her fear of its multi-hued arc that she had held as a girl. Like many Brazilians of African ancestry, she was raised in a household in which Catholicism and African spirituality combine to bring about a hybrid system of beliefs called Candomblé. Candomblé, the Afro-Brazilian religion that is similar in many ways to Spanish Caribbean Santería, or to Franco-American Voudoun, holds that potential spirit allies, or "orixas," were brought from Africa along with the slave population. Ponciá inherits an ancestral ambivalence toward the orixa who is called "angorô" in the Angolan tradition and "Oxumarê" in the Yoruba tradition.

Ponciá's angorô is a sky serpent, the lord of the rainbow and transporter of water between heaven and earth. This celestial messenger can be depicted as both male and female in Angolan imagery. The implication is that of a dual-sexed being, but not necessarily the harbinger of good tidings that is found in Biblical lore. On the contrary, some Central African traditions hold that the rainbow spirit is quite malevolent, as it signals the stoppage of life-giving rains. Still others will describe the sky snake as a duplicitous force that, upon lighting on earth, manifests as the fire entity that ignites the domestic cooking flame. In some Afro-Brazilian "houses"– schools in which Candomblé is practiced – Oxumarê/Angorô is one of the orixa that changes sexes, or is found to spend half the year with a female top and a male bottom, and the other half of the year with a male top and a female bottom. Ponciá's ambivalence toward the rainbow is born of ancient African beliefs that continue to shape her community's ways of knowing the natural world.

Next, readers are likely to be unfamiliar with a species of bird that populates the river of Ponciá's girlhood. The sunbittern, a water-edge bird that hunts along heavily forested rivers and streams, has a long, straight bill, a pointed tail, and short, orange legs used for stalking waterside prey. Her delight in sharing the river with this elusive bird is an example of her harmonious convivial with the forest waters. When she leaves this world behind for the promise of the city as an adult, she abdicates both the large and small enchantments that are central to her emotional prosperity. Her move to the city is indicative of the demographic shifts that have taken place across the Americas in which rural subsistence has been steadily overwhelmed by the draw of new opportunities implied by the metropolis. However, for the rural poor, the move to the city simply means replacing the squalor of the country for the violence and indignities of the "favelas," the Brazilian shanty towns that are devoid of services such as running water, paved streets, and electricity.

After she has spent several years working for middle and upper class employers and living in the favela, Ponciá's return trip to the village of her childhood is a revelation. The city has provided her with new eyes and a critical distance that permit her to witness the fruitless labors of poor, rural blacks as an echo of colonial slavery. She recalls the national liberatory myths of the "Lei do Ventre Livre" ("Law of Free Birth") and the "Lei Aurea" ("Golden Law") that constitute the foundational fairytales on which Brazil has built its self-image as a racial democracy. The Law of Free Birth (literally phrased in English, it is the "Law of the Free Womb") was enacted on September 28, 1871, freeing all children born to slave parents. Next, the Golden Law was adopted on May 13, 1888, abolishing all slavery in Brazil. Both laws were signed by Isabel, Princess Imperial of Brazil (1846-1921), the acting regent on several occasions in which her father, Emperor Dom Pedro II, was in Europe. Ponciá's return to her village concretizes her awareness of race: the persistence of the conditions of slavery and the daily manifestations of racism at every institutional and interpersonal level did not disappear when Princess Isabel waved her "magic wand."

The legislature that was supposed to bring the nation a step closer to racial harmony did nothing to address the fact that Brazil was the last country in the Western hemisphere to abolish slavery, and had only done so under intense diplomatic and economic pressures from an international community that hoped to diminish Brazil's advantages on the world market by disallowing the use of slave labor. Brazil's "Redeemer," as Princess Isabel came to be known, abolished slavery, but at the same gave birth to an empty policy that dismissed the category of race from Brazilian political discourse. Both in the U.S. and in South Africa, systems of demarcation such as Jim Crow laws and apartheid officially excluded blacks from participating in nation-building projects. Brazil had no such set of legislative barriers, and even produced a school of cultural critics led by Gilberto Freyre whose 1933 sociological treatise entitled *Casa Grande e Senzala* (often appearing in English as *The Masters and the Slaves*) proposed a paternalistic celebration of Brazil's tradition of racial "intermarriage." Brazil's official attitude has been to embrace blackness in its international image but to deny African contributions at the local and national discourses of selfhood.

Evaristo's critique of racial disparity reads alongside her efforts to bring the struggles of black womanhood to light. By emphasizing black, feminine ways of knowing, the character of elderly Nengua Kainda offers a solution to the pathologies of both racism and misogyny that plague Latin American society. Figuring prominently at the heart of the novel, Nengua Kainda embodies black spiritual authority and community integrity. Kainda's divinations and her quiet counsel are central to the struggles of Ponciá as well as to those of the girl's mother and brother, providing a vision that reaches as far into an African past as it does into the future prospects of its American descendants.

Toward the end of the story, Kainda is found in repose in a "terreiro," a large indoor or outdoor space that is consecrated for service of the orixas. Her dominion over this house of worship informs the reader of her mastery of Candomblé's mysteries that serve to guide and protect the Vicencio family in all their undertakings. Kainda's works serve to rehabilitate African practices and to refute the colonial messages about authority that sustain patriarchal, neo-feudalistic social orderings.

The characters that Evaristo presents here are shaped by severely limited access to formal education and literacy. The author deals with this paucity of verbal expression by minimizing the use of dialogue, and juxtaposing the silences born of oppression with the silences that spring from Kainda's tradition: a wealthy silence of spiritual acuity that runs beneath the superficial flows of rhetoric and conventional intellect. This hunger for a deeper knowledge base – one that honors ancestral roots and is at the same time capable of empowering the forward-looking imagination – is what drives our heroine's quest.

My final remark deals with the translation of style and tone in black, feminine Brazilian writing. For an English-speaking readership, it is important to understand that a spoken reading of the original Brazilian Portuguese would immediately inform audiences that the novel's "accent" conveys a contentious, marginal relationship to the mainstream usage of Brazilian Portuguese. While a Brazilian reader might immediately recognize the novelistic language as poor and black, a search for similar terminology among U.S. black communities, or the imposition of a given, regional accent would sound forced, provincial and dated, so I have opted to use a more mainstream American English than that found in its Portuguese counterpart. The decision to steer clear of country bumpkin or city slicker vernacular is not an attempt to "elevate" more colloquial registers of speech, but rather to provide enough space for the brogue, drawl, lilt, twang or patois that permits the reader's own identity to be refracted and transformed in the sounds – and silences – of the novel.

Paloma Martinez-Cruz, Ph.D.
North Central College
Naperville, Illinois

Ponciá Vicencio

*P*onciá Vicencio shuddered when she saw a rainbow in the sky. It recalled the fear she had known as a young girl. They said that if a girl passed beneath a rainbow she turned into a boy. She had been on her way to look for clay at the river's edge, and there was the sky snake, drinking water. How would she get to the other side? Sometimes she would remain for hours and hours on the edge of the river waiting for the colored sky snake to disappear. There was no way to cross! Awful rainbow! It was a terrible predicament. But she knew her mother was waiting. So, gathering the folds of her skirt between her legs so that they covered her sex, in a single bound, heart leaping in her chest, she passed underneath the angorô. Afterward, she patted everything with her hands. There were the little breasts that were just beginning to grow. There was the pubis, very flat, without any protrusion other than the hairs. Ponciá felt immense relief. She was still a girl. She had jumped quickly, in a single bound. She had managed to fool the rainbow and had not become a boy.

1

Back then Ponciá Vicencio enjoyed being a girl. She enjoyed being who she was. She enjoyed everything. She enjoyed. She enjoyed the newly cleared land, the river that ran between the rocks, the feet of the sunbittern, the feet of the bitter palm, the stalks and the cornfield. She loved the play she shared with the towering dolls of maize. Ponciá ran and jumped among them. The elements ran at her side. It was a game. The wind would blow in the cornfield, and the dolls would bend to the ground. It would make Ponciá Vicencio laugh. Everything was so good. One day when she was playing this game, she saw a tall woman, so tall that she reached high into the sky. First she saw the woman's feet, then her legs which were long and delicate, and then the body, which was opaque and empty. She smiled at the woman, who returned her smile. It seemed that her mother paid no attention when she told her the story of this tall, transparent woman. But Ponciá noticed that she had been alarmed. A few days after that, when her father arrived, she overheard her mother asking him to cut down the field. He had argued that it wasn't yet time for harvest. But she insisted. When Ponciá Vicencio woke up the next day, the cornfield had been cut. The dead dolls lay on the ground. Still, she looked everywhere for the tall, see-through and hollow woman that had smiled at her from between the spikes of corn.

That afternoon, Ponciá Vicencio looked at the rainbow and felt a wave of fear. It had been so long since she had seen a celestial snake. In the city, after so many years away from the land, she had even forgotten to contemplate the heavens. But today, when she had awakened early in the morning with the

2

familiar ache that filled her chest, without intending to, she had looked up at the sky, as if asking God for help. That was when she felt regret. A beautiful, whole rainbow in the air divided the home of the hanging waters in two. She brushed her hand across her forehead as though attempting to turn off everything that she was thinking. The old fear visited her and persisted in her body. When she was a girl, she thought that crossing under a rainbow could turn her into a boy. Now she knew that she wouldn't become a man. So, why the fear? She was now grown-up, all of a woman! She stared at the rainbow thinking that if she turned into a man, what would it matter? It summoned the thought of the first man she had ever known.

The first man that Ponciá Vicencio had ever known had been her grandfather. His image remained fixed in her mind even more firmly than that of her own father. Grandpa Vicencio had been very old. He was so hunched over that his face nearly brushed the floor. He was tiny like a twig. She was just a little girl at the breast when he died, but she remembered one detail very distinctly: Grandpa Vicencio was missing one of his hands, and he always hid the severed limb behind him. He cried and laughed a lot. He cried just like a baby. He talked to himself, too. The brief time that she had spent with her grandfather proved sufficient for her to have retained certain traces of him. Her memory clung to the tears mixed with laughter, the little amputated arm, and the unintelligible words of her Grandpa Vicencio. One day he had a crisis of such profound tears and laughter, with such happiness, with such bitterness, that he went right into the next world, just like that. She, then just a babe in arms, saw and felt the odor of candles lit the whole night through. She saw the whole arm of the old man folded in front over his chest. She saw the little arm that was cut off. She felt the smell of fried sweet bread, of the fresh coffee that was served to the women and children that were holding wake for the dead. She felt the smell of white rum exhaled from the mouth of the flask and of the men seated outside who held their hats over their chests. Ponciá Vicencio, still at her mother's breast, never forgot the last cry and laugh of her grandfather. She never forgot that, on that night, she, who had seldom seen her father since he was always working in the distant lands of the whites, heard when he told her mother that Grandpa Vicencio had left something for the girl.

There was much commotion on the day that Ponciá Vicencio came down from her mother's arms and began to walk. She, who had until then refused to either sit or crawl, had never done this before. One day, as her mother stood holding her near the wood fire while gazing into the flame's fervent dance beneath the pan, she felt her daughter slip softly from her arms. She saw her forcing the descent down her chest and standing herself up, then begin to walk. The surprise was not so much from the fact that the child had suddenly begun to walk, but rather in the way she had done it. She walked with one of her arms hidden behind her back, and had her little hand closed into a fist as though it were cut off. It had been nearly a year since Grandpa Vicencio had died. Everyone was asking why she walked that way. When the grandfather died, the girl had been so small! How could she imitate him now? It frightened them. Her mother and her godmother crossed themselves when they looked at Ponciá Vicencio. Only her father took it in stride. He was the only one who wasn't scared when he saw the little arm that acted just as though it had been amputated. He was the only one who thought that it was to be expected, this resemblance between the girl and his father.

$\mathcal{P}$oncia Vicencio remembered very little about her father. The man never came home. He was always gone, working the fields that belonged to the whites. There was no time to spend with his wife and children. When it wasn't time to plant, it was time to harvest, and all of his time went to the ranch.

Poncia's father knew how to read all the letters of the alphabet. He knew each one by heart. Wherever he was, he would decipher letters. He didn't, however, know how to piece them into syllables, and much less into words. He had learned to read letters as a game with the young boss. As the child of ex-slaves, he had grown up on the ranch living the same life as his parents. He was the young boss's attendant. It was his duty to play with him. He was the horse on which the youngster would gallop and dream of seeing all of his father's lands. They were the same age. One day the little colonel ordered him to open his mouth because he wanted to make his piss there inside. The attendant opened wide. The other's urine fell hot into his throat and streamed out of the corners of his mouth. Young boss laughed and laughed. He cried and didn't know what it was that salted his mouth more, if it was the taste of urine or the flavor of his own tears. That night he hated his father more than ever. If they were free, why did they have to stay there? Why, then, were there so many blacks in the slave quarters? Why didn't they move on and find other places and different jobs? One day he asked his father this question very carefully, very cautiously. He was afraid of his attacks. His cut off arm, when it struck, weighed heavy like iron. It always landed squarely on its unhappy target. By aiming straight for the face, it would flavor his mouth with blood. He asked, and the father's answer was a rough cackle between a laugh and a wail. The man didn't look at the boy. He looked into time as though combing the past, the present, and the future to find a precise answer, but it was always slipping just beyond his grasp. Attendant to young boss, slave to young boss, everything to young boss, nothing to young boss. One day the little colonel, who already knew how to read, became curious to see if blacks could learn the symbols, the letters of the whites, and began to teach them to Ponciá's father. The child responded quickly to the teaching of the indifferent master. In a short time he learned the names of all the letters. When young boss realized that a black could learn, the game was over. Sure, a black could learn. But what would a black do with the knowledge of whites? The father of Ponciá Vicencio, in the matter of books and letters, never progressed beyond that level of instruction.

$\mathcal{P}$oncíá Vicencio loved to sit by the window looking out into nothing. Sometimes, she became so distracted that she forgot about dinner and when she looked up, her husband was already arriving home from work. She spent all her time with her thoughts, with remembering. She recalled the past life and thought of the present, but she didn't dream about or even invent anything for the future. Poncíá's tomorrow was made of forgetting. In other times, she had dreamt so much! As a child, she had even dreamed up another name for herself. She didn't like the one they gave her. As a girl, it had been her habit to go to the brink of the river, and when she got there, she would look at herself in the waters, shouting out her own name: Poncíá Vicencio! Poncíá Vicencio! She felt like she was calling out to someone else. She never heard a reply to her name from within. She tried others. Pandá, Malenga, Quieti – but none of these seemed like her, either. She, unnamed and trembling with fear, was afraid of this game, but she pressed on. Her head rolled in the void, she felt empty without a name. She was no

9

one. That was when it would seize her, the urge to laugh and cry.

Ponciá's husband entered the house and looked at his distracted wife sitting at the window. His look bore hatred. The woman seemed dim-witted. She spent hours and hours there silently looking out and seeing nothing. She spoke little and when she spoke, it was usually to say something that he couldn't understand. He would ask, and when the answer came, most of the time it made talking to her even more confusing. On one evening, she spent the whole night in front of the mirror calling to herself. She called and called and didn't answer. He was scared, frightened. In the morning, she seemed more upset than ever before. She asked the man not to call her Ponciá Vicencio anymore. Fearfully, he asked her what, then, should she be called. Looking deeply and frantically into his eyes, she told him that he should call her nothing.

Ponciá's husband was tired, very tired. His clothes were filthy just like his body, exuding dust. He and the rest of the crew were tearing down an old house. It was slow work; each hour was spent pounding a mallet and striking the wall that would push back against their force. He dwelled, with each blow, on the tiny shack where they lived, and the way it swayed with the slightest wind. The woman was so far away that he wanted to force her back to earth. He gave her a violent shake from behind, shouting out her name. She returned his look of hatred. She thought about leaving that place, getting out of there, going underneath the rainbow and turning right into a man. But she brought herself to her feet, loathe to abandon her corner, and began to ready his supper.

$\mathcal{B}$ack when Ponciá Vicencio went to the river to peer at herself in the waters, and call out to herself as though she were in front of a mirror, she still had not felt so much sadness in her chest. She had been raised alone, by herself with her mother. She had a brother, but she rarely played with him because he went with their father to work the fields in the lands of the whites. She and her mother went for days and days without seeing the two. During the rains, their visits grew even farther apart. The mother made pans, pots, and animal figurines from clay. The girl would scoop out clay from the river's edge. After they dried, her mother would bake the works in a clay oven. The pieces would then turn hard, strong, and difficult to break.

Ponciá Vicencio was very skilled at working with clay. One day she made a short little man, curved, thin, like a little twig with a cut off hand curled around his back. Her mother snatched the figure away and wanted to smash it, but she forced herself to contain this urge, as well as the scream that welled up inside. In a few days' time, the father returned from the lands of the whites with their provisions. Her mother's heart burned with concern and confusion. What was wrong with that girl? First, she had walked all of the sudden, in the same exact way as the grandfather...Now, she had made the little man from clay, the spitting image of the old man. The piece was wrapped up, and she had hidden it at the bottom of a large trunk. Even so, it seemed that from somewhere inside the trunk sprang laugh-laments, cry-cackles. What should she do with their daughter's creation? What were they to do with the Grandpa Vicencio inside their daughter? Yes, it was him. Precisely him! How did the girl remember him? She had been so small, still at the breast, when the man had passed. How, then, was it possible for Ponciá Vicencio to remember every last aspect of him?

Ponciá Vicencio's father looked at the man of clay that the girl had made and saw his own father. Taking up the work into his hands, he examined it closely. The eyes, the mouth, the curved back, the slenderness, the severed arm – everything was like him, just like him. Laughter played around the mouth, but the face bore an expression of pain. He had the feeling that the man of clay was going to laugh and cry the way his father had. He called the girl and returned the object to her. He made no gesture of approval or reproach. That was Ponciá Vicencio's own work that she had made for herself. Nothing that could be given away or sold. He turned his back on his daughter, and between clenched teeth, muttered to his wife that he couldn't see what the fuss was about.

As for Donciá's father, he could care less if the girl was like his father or not. It was all the same to him. He couldn't think of a time in which he had either loved, or hated, his father. He had other sorts of feelings for him. When still a small boy, he had perhaps felt fear, respect, love. But after what happened, there had been terror, hatred, and shame, most of all shame, when his father had begun to laugh and cry at the same time and to say those witless things. As the old man grew worse, he began to wish desperately that he would die. One day, the thought arose that he could try to kill him. He knew that his life hung by a thread and that just one push would be enough, that just remembering would be enough. He attempted it several times. One day, as the sun descended in the sky, he took his father by the shoulders, shook, shook, and shook. The man laughed and cried desperately. But even that had not brought death. Poncia's father knew, though, how to cut short this old man's life. It was just a matter of making him think about what had happened. He started asking the questions, then stopped. He knew that if he made his father remember everything, if he hurt him in his memory, the man would drop. He would die the death of all deaths, the deepest. He opened his mouth, again forming the words. He stopped. To remember what happened was to sip from death itself – but this death would be his own.

13

$\mathcal{O}$nce the flow of memory thoughts was interrupted, Ponciá Vicencio arose, straightened her back that still smarted from the man's blow, and slowly set out to prepare the food. She looked at him, who had settled on the filthy bed, and was even more disgusted with life. What was she doing at the side of such a man? There was no longer any pleasure between them. She recalled the first time in which she had felt pleasure. She had been about eleven years old. She had just passed beneath the rainbow. Frightened, she lied on ground on the other side, and began to pat herself on her body to see if there had been any kind of change. When she touched there between the legs, she felt a light thrill. She touched again, and even though she had been afraid, it was good. She touched more and more, there inside, and waves of pleasure arrived despite her shock and fear. Above her own body hovered that of the rainbow, a menacing curve, presiding over her.

The man's shout protesting Ponciá's slow pace was what,

once again, interrupted her remembrances. It bothered her, but she said nothing. She swallowed the rage down dry with a gulp of silence. She stirred the beans. The flame danced underneath the pan as though it wanted to set fire to it all. Despite her coming and going in time, his supper was soon ready. She went to the cupboard, took down an empty can of guava paste, and began to serve him. The pan gave off a fragrant smell. She wondered whether or not she would eat. She grabbed a handful of crackling with the tips of her fingers, brought it to her mouth, and began to chew. The man ate on the bed, holding the can in one hand. The food went down wrong, crooked, dry, making him cough between one spoonful and the next. She went to the clay pot and returned with a small cup full of water. He drank it down in a single swallow. He left the can with the rest of the food on the floor. He threw off his shirt and pants. In his filthy smelling underwear, he buried his face in the pillow stuffed with rags and was soon fast asleep.

Ponciá Vicencio's eyes vagrantly drifted around the room where they lived. The dust gathered on the old wardrobe. From the roof's rafters hung an accumulation of spider threads and blackened cobwebs. The piles of dirty laundry grew day after day in the corners of the room. The newspaper pages that lined the shelves of the wardrobe were already yellow with time and gnawed at the edges by rats and cockroaches. Every night she contemplated the neglect of the house, the disorder that was so unpleasant, but she didn't have the courage to change its aspect. She shut her eyes and remembered the little house with the packed earth floor of her childhood. The dirt had been completely smooth, and although it was dry it seemed like it was slick. Everything there was made from earth. Cook pans, cups, ornaments, and even the ladle that her mother used to serve beans. With the recollection of her mother, she felt a tightening in her chest. What had happened to her? Had she died? She had to raise certain stories from the past. But, how? And her brother? She had lived with him only a little when she was a child, a very little, but on their rare occasions together, they had been so happy. They had not shared physical affection, but even so, even without touching or embracing, they loved each other deeply. She knew that he, too, was roaming the world. Would he find it? Was it possible that he had made his way? Or would he be reduced, small, miserable, in some old shack, just like her? Ponciá had woven a web of dreams and now she saw one by one how its strands unraveled, and everything became a great hole, a great void.

On the freshly cleared land, in the home of mud walls and its hard-packed, earth floor, dolls made from corn cobs, the rainbow turned coral snake drinking water from the river, Ponciá loved being a girl, she was happy. The mother never complained of the man's absence. She passed the time singing aloud over her pottery. When he returned, she was the one to decide what he would do around the house. What he would do when he went back to the lands of the whites. What he would tell them. What he had to bring back the next time he came home. She would roll the clay pieces into banana leaves and straw, indicate which ones were to be sold, and stipulated the price. She gave him the names of the people who would receive them as gifts. At times, the father would disagree entirely. About what he would do on his days at home, on the specified prices of the pieces, and about the people who would receive them as gifts. The mother would repeat what she had already said. The father would end up doing what she wanted, and storm off without saying good-bye to her or the daughter, tugging the son by the hand. The mother, from the doorsill, would bless the son and wish in a loud voice for them to go with God. Humming gaily, she would spin back around to greet the home's interior. Panciá Vicencio smiled. Her father was strong, her brother almost a man, and yet their mother was the one to give orders that they would have to obey. It was so good to be a woman! One day she would also have a man who, even when fighting, would have to do everything she wanted, and she would have children, too.

In those times, a group of missionaries made their way to the interior. One day the news broke out. They would stay there and establish a school. Whoever wanted to learn to read could go. Panciá Vicencio received her mother's consent. Who knew — perhaps the girl would find her way out of the fields and go to the city some day. If so, she would need to know how to read. Not in the fields, though! In the fields, a different kind of education was what mattered. On the land, the important thing was to know the phases of the moon, the times for sowing and reaping, the times of water and of draught. The right unguents for skin problems, the remedies for stomach and intestinal problems and feminine discomforts. To know the right conjuring for shingles, for broken or split bones, for children's abdominal pains. The knowledge needed in the fields was different in every way than that of the city. But it was better to let the girl learn to read. Who could say, her path might yet be different.

Ponciá Vicencio applied herself. She learned the alphabet, and recognized letters everywhere. When the father returned, they would read letters together in the primer. As for the father's ability when it came to reading, he had stopped at the point of identifying the letters, but the girl went farther. She began to form syllables, but when she was finally learning to form words, the mission was ended. The fathers went to other towns, leaving common law couples married, little children baptized, older ones having taken first communion, and the sick anointed. The sick who were cured by the elixirs of Nengua Kainda got up from their beds and would find time enough in their lives to sin again.

When the ministers left, their duties complete, Ponciá knew that she could not wait for them to bring her another opportunity to increase her knowledge. She learned by herself, tenaciously making her way through the pages of the primer. And in a few months time, she knew how to read.

*T*ime went by, and the girl grew, but she never grew accustomed to her own name. She still felt that it was an empty name, distant. When she learned to read and write, it became even worse to discover that there was an accent mark over Ponciá. Sometimes, in an act of self-flagellation, she set herself to copy her name and repeat it, in an attempt to locate herself, to hear herself in its echo. It was so painful to write the accent. It was as though she were torturing herself with a sharp blade that pierced her body. Ponciá Vicencio knew that the last name had come to her from a time even before the grandfather's grandfather, the man she had sculpted from her memory into clay, the one that her mother didn't like to see staring back at her. Mother, father – everyone was Vicencio. In its signature lived the reminder of the master's power, of a certain Colonel Vicencio. Time went on and left the mark of those who had become the masters of lands and of people. And Ponciá?

19

Where had Ponciá come from? Why? In what fold of memory would the meaning of her own name be written? To her, Ponciá Vicencio was a name that didn't have an owner.

The girl heard it said at times that Grandpa Vicencio had left an inheritance for her. She didn't know what an inheritance was; she wanted to ask, but didn't know how. Whenever they spoke of him (and they rarely spoke of him, very rarely) the conversation was low, close to a whisper, and when she approached, it stopped. They said that she was a lot like him in every way, even the way she would look at things. They said that she liked to look out into emptiness, just the way he used to. Ponciá Vicencio didn't reply to their talk, but she knew where she was looking. She saw it all, even the emptiness.

When Ponciá Vicencio's father died, the shock was probably even greater than the pain had been. Weeks earlier he had been at home pulling up the weeds that insisted on growing right back, serving as hiding places for the snakes. He had also taken the pottery that his wife had made in order to sell it. He had been well when he left the house. But for missing his wife and daughter (a complaint that never left his lips), it might have been said that he had been happy. Ponciá's father was not inclined to laugh out loud, being a silent type, quiet, who kept his feelings to himself. When he was a boy it hadn't been that way. In spite of young boss's commands and the blind obedience that he was supposed to show, his sorrows would burst forth in immense tears, and his laughs came in raucous shouts. But as he grew older, he gradually learned to disguise what came from within. He no longer cried, and he kept his laughter to himself. The most that he would do, if he was unhappy, was mutter, and this was done in a low voice, with his lips drawn so tightly that the grumbling would smother itself on its own, in a deep, nullified dispute.

One clear afternoon, as the sun cooked the earth and the men toiled at harvest, as they intoned rhythmic verses and the bodies swayed in concert with the day's labor, on that afternoon, Ponciá Vicencio's father was bowed with the rhythm of the music, but he did not gather the fruits of the earth; he surrendered to it. His companions, caught up in their efforts, did not notice. Moments later, in mid-verse, they heard a thud, and then a different marking of time. They were the sobs of Ponciá's brother who was lying across the body of his father as it rested face-down on the ground. Many days, nearly a month later, the boy got up the courage to go home and tell his mother and his sister what had happened. The woman, when she was able to make out that her son was returning alone, ran out to meet him. She took him into her arms, and then, slowly and solemnly, she embraced the emptiness as though someone were there. She asked nothing. She knew. In those days she had dreamed of her husband many times. But she hadn't been able to see his face. This time his back was to her, that time his hat was pulled so low on his head that it covered his face. And one afternoon, when the weather was clear and hot, she heard the verses, cries, and the laments. In these laments, she recognized the voice of her son.

Mother and son returned walking hand in hand. This was the first note of affection that his mother had shared with him since the boy had become a man She squeezed his hand, as

22

though she were afraid of him running away as well. She called the girl and told her that her father would not come back. He had gone on a long journey. Ponciá, at first, was angry. How could the father have done that? She knew people who had gone on the final journey, but they had spent a long time making their farewells. They first tried Nengua Kainda's tinctures. And only after everyone had grown used to the idea of their departure, and they had become accustomed to it themselves, had they taken their leave. Ponciá spent a long time, years, perhaps, waiting for the father to turn up – at any second, for any reason, he might suddenly appear. Perhaps her mother felt it, too, since she always kept her husband's things in their old place. And on the days when the son returned from work, she would wait for him in the doorsill and bless him, then she would take five paces forward, and with a long, firm gesture, she would embrace the emptiness. The woman never believed that her husband was truly gone.

*P*onciá Vicencio lay on her back in the filthy bed at the man's side with her eyes gazing into empty space. She saw the image of pigs in their sty that eat and sleep their whole lives through just to be sacrificed. My God, could this be living? The days passed, she was tired, weak to keep living, but the courage to die – she didn't have that yet, either. Her husband liked to say that she was defeated by her own emptiness. Could it be? It could! At times, she even felt as though her face were a great void, replete with nothing and of nothing.

When Ponciá Vicencio resolved to leave the town where she was born, the decision was forceful and sudden. She was tired of everything there. Of laboring over the clay with her mother, of coming and going in the lands of the whites and coming back empty-handed. Of seeing the lands of the blacks dotted with farms, taken care of by women and children because the men spent their lives working the master's lands, and afterward, the majority of the harvest would be handed right back to the colonels. Tired of the insane struggle, devoid of glory, in which everyone slaved just so they could wake up each day even poorer than the last while others grew wealthy the whole day long, she believed that she might design a different path, invent a new life. Hoping to meet this new future, Ponciá decided to leave by train the very next day since the machine would take such a long time to return to the town again. She didn't even have time to say good-bye to her brother. And now, lying there with her eyes wide open, penetrating the nothing, she asked herself if it had been worth it to leave her land. What had happened to the vivid dreams of a better life? They weren't just dreams, they were truths! Truths that had been emptied the moment she lost contact with her people. And now living dead, she lived.

When the train slowed its march and stopped at the station, Donciá Vicencio squeezed the small bundle of clothes tightly to her bosom that she had been jealously guarding the entire journey. She stood up anxiously and peered pleadingly out of the window. Not devising a single familiar face, she felt a profound sadness, even though she had already known that no one would be there to greet her. She didn't know anyone, had never seen the city before, and all of her relations had remained behind. Not one of them would have risked an adventure of this scale. It was growing dark, and Donciá didn't know what to do. She headed quickly for the exit, and was soon outside of the station. She wanted to look back, but she feared her own desire to retreat. She looked straight ahead and saw an imposing cathedral at the end of the avenue, its lights burning to draw its flock. The clock had an enormous face, and from the distance she managed to read the time. It was six. Donciá was then nineteen years old, pulled towards forms that might produce a sense of security. She walked firmly, one foot in front of the other, only stopping when she had reached the steps of the temple.

The first impression that Ponciá Vicencio had inside the church was that the saints were real. They were as large as the people. They were washed and painted. They seemed to even have been bathed. They certainly must have been more powerful than those from the little chapel were she had been born. The ones from there were tiny and dressed just as poorly as everyone else. When the lights of the candles illuminated their faces, it was possible to see that they had a pained look, desperate, like the sinners poised in litany. Not the saints at this cathedral! These were calm. Ponciá looked at the people around her. They matched the saints, with clean and shining chaplets gleaming from between their fingers. She remembered her own. They were Our Lady's Tears beads. With a quick gesture she drew the dark beads, her body's protectors, from around her neck. She didn't have the courage to expose them in public and worked them down to the bottom of her bundle. She knelt, attempting a Hail Mary.

The inspiration in Ponciá's heart spoke to her of the kind of future her life would hold. Her strong belief proved to be the only practical thing that she had brought with her to help face a voyage that lasted three days and three nights. Despite the discomfort, the hunger, the corn meal pone that ran out on the very first day, the thin coffee stored in the little jug, the pieces of raw brown sugar that she would scarcely lick, not even sucking them, so that they would last until the end of the journey, she still brought hope with her along with the travel ticket. It had been there, yes, to have a hand in designing her destiny.

Ponciá had left her mother sad and alone. Downcast, she complained of how she would miss her daughter when the girl had told her of the unexpected decision to leave. She even warned her of what it would mean to live in the city. Ponciá tried to console her mother by telling her that some day she would return for her and her brother as well. And together, they would all be happy.

Ponciá Vicencio could not understand why the people from the village were so afraid of the city. Some had reached the city and things went just fine for them, but they only remembered, only bothered telling the unhappy rumors, the failures. They were always telling the story of what happened to Maria Pia. The girl had been infected by her boss's son. The boy had been so persistent, speaking only of his love for her. He wanted to, she wanted to. It wasn't necessary for anyone to know – especially not their parents. It could be right there, in her room at the end of the kitchen. And Little Raimundo? He fooled himself with those friends, fell for their talk, and became seduced by the fast money, agreeing to sell everything that they sent his way. He even came to sell some things to the people in the fields. Everything was very fine. Bolts of cloth, wedding and baptismal gowns, work clothes, watches, purses, and even a radio. Later it was discovered that his friends had fled, and he was the one left behind to go to jail.

There were others, story after story about acquaintances that had left the village for the city and were robbed at the station upon arriving. They lost the little that they had, and right there where they landed, were forced into begging. Others didn't find work, or earned so little that they couldn't make a living. And life became worse than it had been in the fields. She knew of many sad situations in which everything had gone wrong. She tried to think of someone that had enjoyed a happy ending. She couldn't recall. She tried harder but just couldn't remember a single one. She didn't become discouraged. They spoke so much and so often of those sad souls that it had become the only thing she could remember having heard. But it didn't matter. In her case, when she went back to look for her loved ones, it would be a story with a happy ending.

*P*onciá Vicencio tried to pray a Hail Mary. The brightness of the church, the pretty music that they sang from high above, the clean robes of the priest, and the beauty of the saints and the women so finely dressed that were at her side – all of it distracted her. She began the prayer several times, always losing herself in the middle of the words. She spent a long time in the church. Everything was so beautiful. God must really like all of the finery.

After a while, the sounds from the chorus began to fade. People were leaving, lights were turned off. When she noticed her surroundings, the church was almost empty – one here, another over there. She tried to concentrate again on the prayer. She shut her eyes and managed to finish reciting the rosary. When she was done, she knew that she had to do something. Leave the church and try to find someplace to sleep. Everything had been resolved so quickly. She had thrown her few things together in a flash, and out of the blue was telling her mother of her sudden decision to leave. It needed to be brief, very brief. She couldn't stay there rehearsing the farewell. The train left early the next day. If she missed that one, the next one wouldn't come for many days, almost a month. She told her mother to give her brother a hug for her; she couldn't go all the way to the lands of the whites to look for him.

Ponciá's mother was incredulous as she listened to the girl talk about her decision to leave. Why such a sudden good bye, as if she was running away? Ponciá couldn't explain that her urgency came from the fear that she might not manage to really go. From the fear of going backwards, of being desperate to escape instead of staying there and repeating her family's story. Now that she was in the city, alone, where would she go? What would she do? She had already lost a lot of time contemplating each detail of external faith there in the house of God. She heard the stirring of heavy doors. The sacristan was closing the church. Bewildered, she set out without knowing which way to turn.

$\mathcal{P}$onciá Vicencio spent her first night in the city right in the church doorway. She saw the sacristan close the door. He noticed her too, tightly clutching the bundle made up of her few belongings to her bosom. She wanted to ask for information, to see the father and beg for the charity of some food and a swallow of water, but could not find the courage.

At certain times in her life she had passed the night in vigil, as when there was a wake for the dead, but she had never been all by herself. She was cold and afraid. In a short while others began to arrive. Beggars, children, women and men. They were happy and smiling, despite the discomfort and cold. Ponciá saw some already spread across the ground, sheltered under newspapers, and a chill crept over her. She thought about the saints that were inside, the candles and the candlestick holders, the stained glass windows, the long pews of lustrous wood. She pictured the smooth floor, shining, almost slick inside the church. She looked around her again, all of them calm, several already sleeping. She opened the bundle, retrieved the chaplet made from Our Lady's Tears, respectfully kissing the dark beads that were diluted by the color of night, crossed herself, and began to say a Hail Mary.

The night was long and cold. The church bell startled Ponciá and her company every time it clanged. She began to recall her childhood, the people from the fields, what had happened to them in life and in death. She remembered the tall, see-through, hollow woman that had smiled at her that day in the middle of the cornfield. She remembered Grandpa Vicencio's wake, the different aromas and the flickering candle. She remembered how she would overhear them saying that the grandfather had left her an inheritance. She remembered how her father had gone away to work and never come back. She still remembered the figure she had shaped from clay, and the way everyone had said it was Grandpa Vicencio. She felt her bundle. What a shame! She had left the clay man at home. All of her mother's anxiety and foreboding that had been thick in the air at the time of her departure appeared before her now. That memory was mixed with the face of her brother, who she had not seen in over a month. She felt a weight in her heart, a deep sorrow, a dark omen. She arose with difficulty. She wanted to go. Where? She sat back down again. A beggar was sleeping soundly beside her, but now and then he would start thrashing his fists in the air. She wanted to be on the train, to be going back. She hid her face in the bundle that was pressed against her breast and very softly, almost silently, almost hidden even from herself, she cried.

33

Ponciá Vicencio awoke to the noise of doors swinging open. The house of faith opened to gather its faithful. Aged women, with the look of sleepwalkers, entered quickly, each one looking as if she wanted to be the first to compliment God. The beggars, that at night had been spread across the steps, curled themselves up more tightly or arose to allow the crowd of contrite faithful to pass inside for the first mass of the day. It was six in the morning. Many of them had begun to disperse, mostly the children. The older ones reclined right there and extended hats or small cans (emptied of guava paste) in which a few coins would occasionally drop. Moved by their fate, Ponciá collected her last coins and dropped them into a few of the cans.

Trying to gather up the courage that was hiding under a blanket of fear, Ponciá prepared herself to ask the ladies leaving the church if they were in need of a worker. With each passing Christian, she made haste to form the question, but her speech remained buried in her throat. When the first one came out, she approached her quickly, but the lady kept going. When Ponciá finally managed to open her mouth, the lady was already far away. And that was how it was with the others. She decided, then, to wait with the words set in order. She moved away from the main door of the church and watched the gathered panhandlers back a few steps away to divide a loaf of bread among themselves. She chose an older woman who looked like her mother to approach for training in the matter of soliciting work. The panhandler looked Ponciá over and smiled, telling her that she didn't have any work for the girl, but, if she wanted, they could beg for alms together. You just needed to close your eyes a little, without squeezing too much, and everyone would give a little help to a blind woman who was so young. Ponciá was shocked to consider such a thing. No, she wasn't blind. She could see with her eyes both open and shut. Ever since she was little, she had been able to see things that no one else knew were there.

Turning to the main door, Ponciá positioned herself once more to observe the crowd. Along came another one of the faithful, whom she approached with stuttering words, finally managing to speak of her need for work. She didn't have experience taking care of rich people's houses, but she was very good at shaping clay. The lady listened patiently to everything and at the end of it told her that she didn't need anyone. Disappointed, Ponciá looked inside the church. Few people were left, only three, and among them only one woman, and it was in her, and her alone, in which Ponciá placed her last hope. Ponciá waited for this last one with the words already trying to break from her lips. She needed to be brief. The lady came out, and she touched her arm. She explained that she was just arriving at the capital. She had come by train. The train that went through the town "Vicencio Village." She was looking for work. The lady looked her over from head to toe. She said she wasn't looking for anyone, but her cousin might be. She wrote the address on a little piece of paper and then read it out loud for Ponciá Vicencio, telling her to go there, that very morning. Ponciá, before setting out to find the place, read and reread the writing on the slip of paper:

She folded the paper right away and hid it in her breast. She was thrilled at that moment – she knew how to read.

It only took a short time for Ponciá to get a feel for her new work. She lived in the house of the lady's cousin. She was learning how to manage the affairs of a proper city residence. She never forgot the day when the lady of the house asked her to get a peignoir, and, promptly fulfilling this request, offered the lady the soap bowl. She made plenty of mistakes, but she learned a lot, too. Her heart was light in discovering that life had provided a way out. She would work, save up money, buy a little house, and go back and find her mother and brother. Life had become possible, even easy.

$\mathcal{P}$onciá Vicencio's husband shifted in their bed. The motion made its way to the core of the torpor in which Ponciá found herself, awaking her from her reflections. At her side, he exuded tranquility, as though he was reconciled with his life. My God, could it be that he didn't want anything else? Was he really satisfied with the little shack, the food from the empty guava can? The dust, the dirt from the public constructions, the swallow of rum on the weekends? Swapping a word or two with friends? Could it be that these few things were enough? Sometimes, she caught a glimpse of sadness. At those times she wanted to open her chest, to loosen speech, but the man was such a brute, so silent. Not even when they met, not even back when he smiled and they had still loved, had Ponciá ever been able to open something other than her legs for him. At times she tried, but he was always closed, quiet, dull. Often, pleasure wasn't even shared. Afterward, by herself, she remembered in her thoughts and in her hands the pleasure she had discovered

on that day when, in fear and despair, she had touched herself
to see if she, after going underneath the angorô, was still a girl
after all.

$\mathcal{O}$n the first few occasions in which Ponciá Vicencio had felt the emptiness inside her head, she had been puzzled when she came to. What happened? How long had she been in that state? She tried to remember the events but she could not piece together how things had come to pass. She only knew that, from one moment to the next, it had been as if a hole had opened of its own accord, forming a great fissure both inside and outside of her, a void with which she was confused. And yet, she continued just the same, aware of her surroundings. She saw life and the way in which others transformed themselves; she observed the movements of others that expressed their completion, but she was lost, she was unable to know herself. In the beginning, when the void threatened to overtake her, she was racked with fear. Now, she liked the absence, covered herself with it, with unknowing herself, becoming a distant figure to her self.

Accustomed to owning few possessions, Ponciá Vicencio managed to work and save money toward the purchase of a little house. She wrote often to her mother and brother. Since they did not know how to read, and the postman did not visit the lands of the blacks, she could never be sure that they had received her news. On days in which the freight train that passed through Vicencio Village pulled into the station, the girl hastened there to anxiously search for the familiar face of some adventurer that might have come to the city. A long time had now passed since she had left the land, and she missed dearly the ones that had remained behind. She wanted to go home, but how would she tell her employer? On the other hand, she had to keep the promise that she had made to herself that she would go back for her family.

On these wanderings about the station, years and years later, she learned what had happened. Her brother had also left the village and had come to the same city. Their mother, not wanting to remain alone, had shut the door of the house, rid herself of all of her things, and had gone in search – of who knew what. Of the children, of clay...

A sharp remorse filled Ponciá Vicencio's bosom. Yes, it was she who had caused all of this. She had been the one to leave home first, and now her brother was lost in the city and her mother was left to wander aimlessly in the village. She needed the two of them with her, and the money that she had was already enough to begin to pay for a little home on the outskirts of the city. But why a house now? Would she live alone? This had never been her plan. She needed urgently to find her mother and brother. That was when she was struck by an idea, a solution. She was going to find the local radio broadcasting station and call out to them both. And now and then, she would listen in near despair to the echo of her own troubled voice in its attempt to locate her family. An answer would have to arrive someday, but until that time, Ponciá held onto the hope of seeing them again one day.

When Ponciá Vicencio, after many years of work, managed to buy a little room on the periphery of the city, she went back to the village. The train was the same, with the same difficulties and discomforts. She stepped down into the village's station and walked the rest of the way, hours and hours on foot. She crossed the lands of the whites, tract after tract of earth that had been tamed from the ground up by men that worked there, far away from their families. Ponciá remembered her father, his absences during the long periods of work. She then crossed the lands of the blacks and despite the efforts of the women and young children that maintained them, the fields there were much smaller and the final product was to be divided with the colonel.

Long, long ago, when the blacks had first received those lands, they believed that they had been winning their freedom. Lies. Their situation had changed very little over time. The lands had been offered by the old owners, who said they were giving the gift of liberation. They could stay there to build their dwellings and plant their sustenance. There was only one condition, and it was that they had to continue to work the land for Colonel Vicencio. There was joy in the hearts of many: they were going to be free, to have homes out beyond the master's ranch, to have their own lands and their own crops. For some, Colonel Vicencio was like a father, a God. Time went by and there were the former slaves, now liberated by the "Lei Aurea," their children, born to "free wombs" and their grandchildren, who would never be slaves. All dreaming under the spell of a freedom granted by a princess, a fairy godmother, who, from the ancient whip, had fashioned a magic wand. Everyone still under the yoke of a power that, like God's, was eternal.

After several hours of walking, it felt to Ponciá Vicencio that time's iron hands were frozen against its march in that place. A regent's will had rendered an ancient condition eternal. Many times her eyes witnessed the repeated image of a black mother surrounded by children. The curtain would rise again and again on the scene of little ones, children that, with spade in hand, toiled in the labors of the fields.

Ponciá Vicencio's little house of mud and sticks was still standing. The rains had begun and green growth threatened the structure from all sides. She was afraid of snakes hiding in the underbrush, but she forged ahead. She pushed through the door that swung open in a welcome that was sweet and slow, as if the house had been waiting to greet her. The packed earth floor was still clean. The little clay vessels that her mother had made were arranged in a row on the shelf. Above the wood fireplace were the coffee mugs that belonged to her father, mother, brother, and her. Forgetting that life had passed them by, they waited meekly as though they were longing for something to drink. Ponciá ran and opened the wooden window. A wind full of verdure, earth, and rain invaded the home. With a full heart, she was once more a part of that space. She continued looking over and picking up the objects that were so familiar to her. She went to the old wooden trunk, removed some of the dry straw from within, and saw, there at the bottom, the man of clay. Grandpa Vicencio looked up at her as though he were asking a question.

Ponciá Vicencio withdrew the clay man from the trunk and set him on the table. She was tired, hungry, raw, and cold. Her head nodded. She sat down quickly on a wooden stool. That was when she saw the deep absence, the profound removing of her self.

When Ponciá came back to herself, it was already almost midnight. How long had she been there? She wasn't sure. She had arrived at midday and now night had fallen. She remembered the fried biscuits that her mother used to make. She opened the bundle (the same as the one she had when she left) and withdrew a meal of bread and sausage. She ate her dinner and wished that there was something for her to drink. She savored the tongue's memory of her mother's coffee. She gazed at the clay man and felt that she was on a precipice, that she might fall into gales of sobbing and laughter.

Remembering the tears-laughs of her grandfather, Ponciá thought about the story that her brother told her after their father had died. When he told it, he had instructed her not to bring it up with their mother. It was the story of Grandpa Vicencio's cut off arm.

Grandpa Vicencio had been born just fine, with whole legs and arms. The cut off arm was from after, in a moment of revolt in which he had begged for death.

When it happened, it was an ordinary day, with all of the men and many of the women working the land. The sugar cane grew and made the owner rich. The sugar fields made the master strong and prosperous. Blood and cane juice might as well have been the same. Grandpa Vicencio and his wife and children had lived for years and years working in those fields. Three or four of his own, born of "free womb," had been sold like so many others. One night, his despair got the best of him. Grandpa Vicencio murdered his wife and then tried to take his own life. Armed with the same sickle that he had used on his wife, he severed his own hand. They stopped him and kept him from going through with it. He was mad, crying and laughing at the same time. Grandpa Vicencio did not die. Life kept going for him, whether he wanted it to or not. They wanted to sell him. But who would buy a crazy slave with a cut off hand? He became a hindrance to the masters. He fed on their leftovers. He ate the dogs' scraps when no one was there to take care of him. And he kept on living, year after year. He would see, through tears and laughs, their suffering, their pain. And only when he was done with laughing out all of his insane laughs and bellowing his mad sobs, did Grandpa Vicencio finally find calm. Ponciá Vicencio had been small, very young, just a babe at the breast.

$\mathcal{D}$awn's light drew another one of Ponciá Vicencio's sleepless nights to a close. Lying with her eyes wide open, she had held vigil throughout the nocturnal hours. She counted the holes in the walls and ceiling. She recognized the lizards that fought over spiders and mosquitoes. She made out the noises of the rats. She heard the amorous moans of the couple that lived in the shack on the other side of the wall.

As morning approached, the nearby chorus of infants that awoke to complain of hunger or cold suddenly invaded Ponciá's ears. She remembered the seven children that she had brought into the world, all dead. Some had lived for a day. She never quite understood why they had all died. The first five had been born at home with the midwife Maria da Luz. The woman had wept with her over the loss of the newborns, so small, that would never grow. The last two had been born in the hospital. The doctors told her that they died because of a blood disorder. After those seven, she never became pregnant again.

Ponciá's husband also mourned the loss of the children. With each unsuccessful pregnancy, he took to long bouts of drinking and avoided her completely. Afterward, he would come back and say that he would make another child and that this one would be born, grow up, and become a man. Ponciá was beyond all hope. She opened her legs, having relinquished pleasure, having abandoned any prayer that it might bring them a child.

Her husband tossed about violently in their bed. He opened his eyes, looked at Ponciá, and shook his head in mute reproach when he realized that she had spent yet another night without sleep. He was uneasy. He wanted to slap her, but he could tell that she was just as apathetic, just as distant as ever, and resolved instead to give her a nudge with his foot. Ponciá awoke from her isolation. She arose as though unaware of his presence, filled the can with water, and turned the ashes of the fire to find the log that she had banked the previous night. Just like on the land, even though the convenience of matches was available, she preferred to bank the fire under the ashes to light it again the next day. She paused for an instant near the fire, watching the boiling water, forgetting that it was time to make the coffee. The man coughed outside in the latrine, and she responded to this call. She prepared the strainer with the remaining dust. The timid scent of the beverage filled the room. She served him the thin drink and a piece of boiled manioc from the previous day. Ponciá remembered how her mother had prepared biscuits for her father and brother when they traveled to work in the lands of the whites. She remembered the care with which she had packed the clay objects. She would wrap everything up in banana leaves and dry straw and give them to her husband to sell at the ranch. She remembered being small and dreaming of growing up and having her own husband and children. There she was now with her husband, no children, and no idea where to find the joy that was evading her. Perhaps it was not his fault; maybe it was her, all hers. He had never changed. All those years he had been quiet, going back and forth between work and home, doing the same thing every day. When there was no work to be found, he was stuck at home or in the neighborhood bar. He drank, but not a lot. He had a low tolerance; it didn't take a lot for him to get drunk. Lately he was often angry with her, letting loose a shower of blows and kicks over the slightest thing. He was always saying that she was going crazy. But in the morning when he got up and waited for his lunch tin, when he drank the thin swallow of coffee (even when the tin was filled to the brim with powder, the drink was always thin), he was calm, almost sweet. He missed the other Ponciá Vicencio, the one he had met that day. Confused, he would wonder what was becoming of his wife. She had been so hard working, , taking such care of everything. She who had left the house with him so many times in the daily labors of tending the fire, cleaning, washing loads of laundry in rich people's houses. What was happening to Ponciá Vicencio?

In the morning, when he and Ponciá left for their jobs, she would watch him walk down the hill and feel a pang in her heart. No, he wasn't happy either. She thought about doing what she could to ease his pain. She could at least make their home a more pleasurable place to live. But how – where would she find this pleasure? Sometimes she mused over which of them had it worse. The woman or the man? She remembered her father, the story of his father, Grandpa Vicencio, of her brother that had worked on the lands of the whites from the time he was a young child and had never had the chance to play. She finally concluded that, at least for the men that she knew, life was just as difficult for them as it was for women. In that moment she was flooded with good intentions. She was going to muster up the strength to change everything. Today, now! But when she came to, she did not know how to explain it. She found herself quiet, sitting in her corner, looking through the window at the changing time outside, while coming and going in the time that went by there inside of her memory.

$\mathcal{O}$n the day that Ponciá Vicencio went back to the land, she had been overcome by the deep emptiness, and thought that it would be best to spend the night right there, in her family home. The beds of branches with their straw mattresses were still in the same place in the other room of the house, the room where she and her mother had slept after her father's passing. Her brother, when he came home, had the bed in the corner of the kitchen, close to the fire. She thought of how she and her brother had slept in the same bed together when they were smaller. Afterward, when he had grown older and was going with their father to work in the lands of the whites, a bed was made just for him, but he preferred the old one. When he came home with their father, he would fight with Ponciá over the bed in the corner. The heat emanating from the fire gave off a feeling of comfort and safety. She also remembered that their father and mother would talk in their room until late. The only sound that could be heard from their father was the rumbling response of hum, hum, hum... That was when Ponciá began to think that men were all but mute. Her brother spoke, but it seemed like he was going mute as well. With each homecoming he spoke less and less, and after their father was gone, it was as though the spirit of speech was gone from her brother, as well. He did, however, sing a lot, just like their father. The man would intone the verses of several beautiful chants and her brother would accompany him. Sometimes, their father sang a few verses and the boy would respond with others. Their mother often spoke, but she liked to sing, too.

Ponciá Vicencio did not sleep that night. Instead, she was consumed by the emptiness, and when she returned she found herself lying down, but alert. She heard footsteps coming from the kitchen. She felt the smell of fresh coffee and corn pone that their mother made. She listened to the rustling her brother made when he rose several times in the night to relieve himself outside by the chicken coop. She heard the roosters' crow before dawn in the empty coop. She listened intently, and what she heard most of all, what resonated most clearly, were the tear-laughs of the clay man.

Early the next day, Ponciá Vicencio got up to find coffee. The can was in its place, on top of the hearth, but it was empty. She started. In the night she had felt certain that the house was inhabited and full of life. Overwhelmed by this feeling, she held still for a brief moment. She expected to see her mother walk through the door with a large clay pot and send her to the river to fetch water.

Something stirred in the hearth from beneath the cookstones, in the midst of ashes. It awakened Ponciá to the present. She saw neither the fire nor the lit kindling logs that her mother used to bank under the ash. A snake slithered slowly through the hearth. Ponciá saw the animal but didn't care to do anything about it. That was when she finally understood that the house was empty. The pain of her mother and brother's absence struck her deeply. She looked at the wooden table and there was the clay man stuck between his cries and laughs. She took up the figure and rolled it, as her mother had done, in a banana leaf packed with straw, stowing him affectionately in the bottom of her bundle. Her memory brought forth the day on which Grandpa Vicencio had died. She had been very small, still at the breast, when she heard her parents say that he had left an inheritance for her.

Ponciá Vicencio pressed her bundle to her chest and gave the hearth another glance. The snake was tranquil, coiled up inside. Ponciá left slowly, pulling the door gently shut behind her so as not to awake anyone within. The sky was dark, it was sure to rain. She didn't know where she would go. It would be nearly four weeks before the train came that would take her back to the city. Meanwhile, she couldn't stay there, at home, without her mother or father or brother or even her grandfather. At night they had been with her the entire time, but during the day, when Ponciá was searching, when she looked, everything had been empty. She couldn't stand to feel their absence in the game of hide and seek that they were playing.

The train that would take Ponciá Vicencio back to the city would not come back for a long time. What would she do? She could work for a few days in the lands of the whites. She hadn't learned how to till the soil for planting, but she knew how to do other tasks that she had picked up in the city. She thought about making pottery to sell, but she would have to go back to the house, go back to the river...She didn't want to do that. There were other homes aside from hers. The other family members were scattered throughout the village. Everyone there was related. Since the first days when black people had been given those lands, no one else had arrived and they had married amongst themselves. They were all relations, maybe since always, from before the time they left the other place. She decided that she would go find the others, who were also her people.

The homes in the lands of the blacks, to a stranger's eye, all looked the same. Smooth and slippery packed earth floor, walls of packed mud and twigs and a thatched roof. The adults' and children's beds were all mats made from tree branches that men and women tied together with vines. The straw-filled mattresses were sometimes perfumed with rosemary leaves that were strewn among the branches. The large iron or clay casks and the great bowls in which the women made sweets yielded great abundance. The children loved to scrape the bowls, savoring the sweet taste of papaya, citron, banana, guava, milk, pumpkin, and brown sugar molasses. They had to be quick. When the bowls were completely cool, green tinted rust stains would appear around the edges that mothers said were poisonous, curbing the children's happy feeding spree with caution.

Children, youths, women, men, the elderly, images of the past were presented before Ponciá Vicencio's eyes as she walked. She had not realized that she had been suffering from homesickness for a long, long time. Ponciá loved the elders, but she also feared them. The white hair, the hoarse voice, the dull eyes gazing into a pool of life stirred by memories. She looked at them from a distance. After having been away for so long, Ponciá met with Nengua Kainda. The tall, thin woman now seemed taller and thinner than ever. She stood straight, despite the years, like a dry palm. The skin of her face, hands, neck, and bare feet were wrinkled like ripe passion fruit. Her eyes were sharp, discerning all. The elder rested her hand on Ponciá Vicencio's head and told her that, although she had not found her mother or brother, she was not alone. That she had to do her heart's bidding. Go or stay? She alone knew, but, wherever she went, the inheritance that Grandpa Vicencio had left her would be with her always. And sooner or later, it would indeed unfold, and the law would be honored. None of it made any sense to Ponciá. She said nothing. Asking for Nengua Kainda's blessing, she prepared herself to move forward in her life.

onciá Vicencio, lost in her musings in the corner by the window, had forgotten the great sense of purpose that had filled her that morning. She had firmly resolved to leave her thoughts aside; to try hard to make changes in her life. But she had not noticed nor could she recall the precise moment in which she had deposited herself there – it had to have been before the first swallow of coffee – to begin searching through her memory for a time gone by. She remembered what Nengua Kainda had said when she had gone back to the village to search for her family. Nengua had told her that wherever she went, whatever she did, the inheritance that Grandpa Vicencio had left would find her. Ponciá had been hearing these words since she was a young girl. What had her grandfather left behind that might belong to her?

Since she was a little girl, she had also heard them say that the lands that the first Colonel Vicencio had presented to the blacks at the time of their liberation had been much more numerous, and that, little by little, they had been taken back by his descendants. A few of the blacks, when the colonel had given them the lands, asked him to write the gift down on a piece of paper and sign it. This was done for a handful. They had displayed their papers for some time, until the day on which the very one who had bequeathed them offered to store the titles himself. He said that when it came to blacks, it would be easy for the paper to be ripped, lost, or who knew what else... The blacks delivered their papers, some distrusting, others trusting. The colonel put away their papers, never again to be placed in black hands. Meanwhile, the lands went back to the whites. Whites that had made themselves masters in former times.

Ponciá's family received one of those papers. The colonel called Grandpa Vicencio, who was already mired in his ways of crics and laughter. The man put the paper the colonel had requested in his mouth between clenched teeth and took it to the colonel. And then, right in the presence of the one who had given it, his amputated arm behind his back, he used his other hand to rip the whole thing to pieces in quick and frenzied movements. At the time, Ponciá's father had been a young man, still without a mate or a wife. She hadn't even been dreamt of back then... So what could the inheritance be that Grandpa Vicencio had left for Ponciá that she had heard them talk about since she was a little girl?

When Ponciá Vicencio spent those days in the lands of the blacks, she visited in the homes of several families. In each of them she found clay pottery that she and her mother had made. And everyone that Ponciá spoke with observed the same thing. She was the spitting image of Grandpa Vicencio. Her way of walking, her arm tucked behind with the hand curled shut as though it were cut off, even the features of the girl's face. It was true, even from a young age, she was the living echo of the old man reverberating in time. She also heard the painful history several times, one she knew well, of the death of her grandmother by her grandfather's hand. She remembered his hopelessness and his madness. They spoke of how her father had hated Grandpa Vicencio for killing his mother. Ponciá knew these stories, and plenty more, but she heard everything as though for the first time. She drank in the details, painstakingly patching together the broken web of the past like someone recuperating a first garment so that they would never again be hopelessly naked.

While waiting in the village for the train's return, she felt the emptiness several times, the absence of her self. She would fall half dead, swooning, still experiencing the world around her, but not situated there, not feeling its emotion. No one feared them; no one was upset by her absences.

When the train finally came through Vicencio Village it peered from around the bend and approached the station at a slow crawl. Ponciá boarded and took her seat. Her feelings were confused. She didn't want to leave, she didn't want to stay. There, her house had been emptied of both its living and its dead. At home, if she had felt the same stirring inside of her at the break of day as she had the night before, she might have remained. She had gone back to look for her family. If they had been there and hadn't wanted to come, who knew, she might have stayed. But she hadn't found anyone. She only felt them at night, but she had needed them throughout the day, as well, every day and always. It was necessary, then, to keep going in order to discover where they had made their new home. She had to find the living and dead somewhere in the world. She was alone; she was empty.

The trip seemed longer and more painful than it had been the first time. But this time, she already had guaranteed work in the city, and had even managed to save enough to put something down on a little house on the hill. And what was more, she was beginning to have a different sort of feeling. She was quite taken with someone she had met in the city. It was the first time.

$\mathscr{T}$his person that Ponciá Vicencio had fallen in love with was a man that worked in civil construction near her own job. And he loved her, too. He saw how alive she was, always working hard to make things happen. She was pretty. She had a curious presence that he couldn't quite figure. She loved to sing. She had the voice of a mother lulling her child to sleep or of a woman making her man happy. They had spoken a few times. He knew that the girl had come from the country and had left her mother and brother, people that she now searched for all the time. She worked there and had a home on the hill. He liked her persistence and the way she looked ahead. She was a woman alone in the world, yet she was much stronger than he. That was exactly what he needed. He also worked, but the problem was that by himself, he didn't know how to dream. She, on the other hand, was a lady who lived in dream, always in some far away place. Sometimes, it was as if her spirit ran away and left her body behind. He respected her, but feared her, too. He didn't pry. After she returned from her visit to the village and hadn't found out anything about her mother or brother, she became even more distant. It was after they had met. One day she showed him a clay man that she had made when she was a girl. She had brought it just then, from that journey home where she spotted it, where she had left it behind. It had been made with skill. But he was afraid of looking into the face of that little statue, and a shudder ran through him when Ponciá kissed the head of that person she had made from clay. He cocked his head at the figure in her hand. It had an arm bent behind it with a closed hand as though it were cut off. She looked so much like the clay image that she was preparing to store. She always held her arm behind her back, and a closed hand as though it were cut off. He asked if she could put her souvenir away so they could get back to their conversation. But neither of them remembered what they had been talking about before. She remained empty for several long moments, her gaze fixed as she whispered unintelligible words. He wanted to touch her, call her, shake her, but he was afraid, terrified of nearing the void that belonged only to her.

*P*onciá Vicencio believed that men seldom spoke. Her father and brother had been examples of men's state of near muteness in the domestic sphere. Now her own man, the quiet one there that she had, confirmed this. What was necessary for him was very little, much less than what she needed. How many times had she wanted to hear, for instance, whether his day had been hard, if the small wound on his forehead had been caused by a brick, or if he had begun the new construction. Many times she had wanted to talk about silly things, like the craving for fried eggs that she had felt during each of her pregnancies. She wanted to confide in him about the old fear that would sometimes visit. She wanted to know if he also had these frights, if he also bore the weight of past suffering. She wanted him to tell her of dreams, plans, hopes that he held for his life. But he was all but mute. He didn't cry, didn't laugh. From the beginning, when she first opened up to him, he would grow mute, lock up his conversation, refuse to make a single gesture that would speak to her. And so, Ponciá was caught in the grips of anxiety and frustration in her attempts to find him. A combination of anger and disappointment would take control of him, and she realized that the two of them would never go beyond the body, that they would never touch each other on the other side of their skin.

*A*fter cleaning the last step of the station's entrance, Luandi stood aside to let Soldier Nestor pass. Luandi admired Soldier Nestor. To Luandi, he was better than the clerk, better than the examiner, better than the police officer, better than God. Soldier Nestor was a black man. A black man and a soldier. Whether he was marching or out of uniform he was always handsome and sharp. And he could read. He would sign his name fast and it would come out just right. One day, Soldier Nestor sent Luandi out to the local bar. He wrote a note asking for a pack of cigarettes that he would pay for later. The owner gave Luandi the requested pack and said to give Soldier Nestor a message. That he come right away and settle the account. Luandi saved the note that Soldier Nestor had written as a souvenir. He delivered the cigarettes but not the barkeeper's message.

Luandi had already been in the city for some years. He had arrived by himself. When he got there, he thought that all he had to do was show up anyplace and offer his services. In the fields that was how it had always worked. If they weren't sowing, then there was harvesting to be done or land to plow, or he would stock the ranch's storehouses. And then there was cane to be milled and coffee to roast. Sometimes he would rope cattle and mend fences. He was a jack-of-all-trades. He did everything. There, in the city, he was learning how to do every kind of job as well. When he first arrived he had no idea about how to get his bearings. He had lost his sister's address on the way. That first day was wet, cold and so very hungry.

The rain dampened Luandi's spirits. His clothing stuck to his body and the wet shoes bothered his feet. It was the first time in his life that his feet had been shod. In the fields his feet had always touched the earth. Here, the lampposts that were always trying to suppress the dark of nightfall disgusted the boy deeply. "Why have I come to the city?" He had muttered to himself between clenched teeth, just as his father had always done. "Why have I come to the city?" The question was asked again. To look for my sister, to make some money, and to grow very rich. Yes, he had to make money. They said that in the city, people needed to work hard, but they did manage to get rich. And when it came to work, Luandi was far from being timid. He splashed into a puddle and was soaked through to the hem of his pants. He felt a stab in the pit of his stomach from hunger. He dug his hand into his pocket, his fingers scraping the contents at the bottom. There was nothing left, not even a last little coin. He leaned up against a wall and tried to open his cardboard suitcase. This was not necessary. The suitcase, completely soaked, split open of its own accord. The youth made a small bundle from the clothes he withdrew. A new pair of pants, and the two old shirts with threadbare cuffs and collars (that had belonged to their father), rolling tobacco, papers for cigarettes and a jackknife. He put the tobacco, papers, and knife in his pocket, leaving the rest of the suitcase to be washed away by the downpour's current. His stomach was still grinding against emptiness. And now? Where would he find his sister? The rain poured insistently. In the fields he only had to look in the village and if he didn't find who he was looking for, someone or other would show up who could help him. Either they would have news or they would offer to take a message to the one he sought. But he knew what he had to do. The next day he would have to walk the entire city. So many had left the fields and were now there! For certain, if he didn't find Ponciá right away, he would find someone who could tell him of her whereabouts.

Luandi didn't have anyplace to spend the night, and after walking for a while, he decided to go back to the train station. He could find a place to sit or maybe lie down on one of the benches to wait for the next day. But he was soon awakened from the middle of a dream by a soldier: What are you doing here? Can you show me your identification? What do you do? Are you carrying a weapon? Luandi told him that he hadn't yet found a job. He didn't have any identification. He had just arrived from the country. And that was when he was searched: in his pocket was the jackknife. He was armed! "I think you should follow me to the station." Soldier Nestor took Luandi by the arm and escorted him out. He had a firm grip on Luandi's arm. They passed a city employee who stared at them while he cleaned the floor. He was black, too. Luandi was fearful, but not in the least bit angry. He was happy. He had just made a discovery. The city truly was better than the fields. There was the proof. A black soldier! Ah! How beautiful! In the city, a black man could give orders, too!

Luandi spent the rest of the night in a cell at the station. Upon arriving, the black soldier summoned another soldier. A white soldier came. He ordered the white man to guard Luandi in his cell. Just lock him in, nothing else... Luandi concluded that the black soldier was quite important. He was the one in charge. The next day he was put before a white man that sat behind a desk and asked him a whole bunch of questions. Where was he from? What had he been doing? Who were his parents? Did he read and write? What kind of job was he looking for in the city? Luandi responded that he had never been to school. He would do any kind of work. He was surprised and confused by the officer's words until he heard him saying:

"Mr. Luandi José Vicencio, you are hereby employed. Right here at the police station."

"Employed? How? Doing what? Wearing a uniform? Being a soldier?"

Peals of laughter rang from the police officer, the black soldier, and the white one. When they were again quiet, it was the black soldier who approached and said his name was Nestor and that if Luandi wanted, he could have a job. It would mean sweeping, cleaning, and servicing the washroom at the police station. Since he didn't know how to write or make his signature, he couldn't become a soldier. But, if he studied a little, it was possible for him to become a soldier one day. And he could go even farther than that, much farther. As he listened, Luandi determined that he only wanted to be a soldier. He wanted to give orders. Make arrests. Pummel. He wanted to command in a loud and forceful voice, just like whites.

On Luandi José Vicencio's first day of work at the police station, a young boy was brought in on robbery charges. He was still a kid, vaguely mulatto with blue eyes who had been pilfering around the Spaniards' store right by the station. The kid swore by everything under the sky that he hadn't tried to steal anything. He swore on his mother's life and he swore by Christ's wounds. The police officer laid into him with his shouting. But Soldier Nestor stood calmly by, impassive, occasionally stroking the end of his baton. The officer concluded his sermon by telling the boy that if it were up to him, he would cut the hands off of every last thief. But just this once, he would order Soldier Nestor to let the boy go.

When he heard the officer talking about cutting hands off, Luandi was taken back to the time of his childhood. Before him appeared the figure of his grandfather with his hidden, cut off limb, laughing-crying-talking to himself. For the first time in his life the thought of his grandfather was retrieved with affection.

His father had not cared for Grandpa Vicencio. He even said that the old man was crazy, a murderer. He had killed his wife and afterward was about to kill himself, and would have done so if he hadn't been stopped in time. Luandi also knew that Grandfather had done it in a moment of madness. He didn't want to be a slave any longer. And what kept him from killing Luandi's father, when his father had been a young boy, was that the boy had been able to run away and search for help. Grandpa Vicencio had wanted to die. If he could not live, then what remained was to die. Luandi's father held on to that picture in his mind of his blood-soaked mother, dead. And he held it throughout his life as a hatred for his father, even though he knew that the man had been deranged, driven mad.

Luandi had worried about being trapped in Grandpa Vicencio's world, but he was now relieved, because he could finally see that the days of slavery were now past. That kind of suffering was only kept alive in the country. In the city, everyone was equal. There were even black soldiers!

Luandi José Vicencio liked working at the police station. The thing he liked the most was the arrival of the convicts. Some would arrive confused and afraid, while heavy hatred was etched into each feature of others. He would look into the faces of each of them, trying to determine which ones were innocent and which were guilty. Sometimes he had the impression that they were all innocent, but at the same time completely culpable. He felt a dull ache in his heart. He, too, was imprisoned within each and every one of them.

A great wanting filled up Luandi's chest. He would learn to

read so he could one day become a soldier. He remembered the missionaries that had spent time in their village. That was when Ponciá had learned to read. He was already going with his father to work the land. And his sister? By then he had already turned over the four corners of the city, seeing all the young black women, looking for the face that was hers. His sister that knew how to read, what had become of her life? Ponciá worked the clay so well. She had expert fingers; they were sculptors of beautiful things, even lovelier than those their mother had made. And their mother? Surely she would still be in their lands, working with clay. Now she was the one who would have to go to the ranch, the land of the whites, talking along the way to the blacks that she would meet. Yes, their mother would most certainly be longing for them, but this was just fine. The day would soon come when he would know how to read, he would become a soldier, he would go back to Vicencio Village and find their mother. And together both of them would find his sister. Where could Ponciá be? And was it possible that her inheritance had already been claimed?

When Ponciá Vicencio awoke on her first morning back from visiting her birth place, an insistent itching emanated from between her fingers. These she scratched until they bled. She set herself to handling the mistress' affairs, but was continually interrupted in her labors by the need to immerse her hands under cool water in the hopes that this would alleviate her torment. In her lifetime she had never had any troubles with her skin at all. When she was born, they had bathed her with armadillo blood to immunize Ponciá against plagues of this sort. So then, why now, already fully grown, was this irritation developing that tickled so much between the fingers? Ponciá Vicencio smelled her hand, and detected the fragrance of clay.

For Ponciá, the city no longer held any grace, and life marched onward without apparent design. She had worked, she had managed to save up a small amount of money with which to buy a tiny house, but her family was gone. She had gone back to the land with the hope of finding some vestige of her mother or brother but had only been able to confirm that they had both disappeared. What could be done now? She had lost the link to the living and the dead. What did the little house matter now? Who would she bring inside to make it a home? Who among the dead or living? She ran into the house where she worked, all the way back to the maid's room, and took the clay man out of her bundle. She held the work to her nose, and it was the same aroma that came from her hand. Ah! So that was it! It was Grandpa Vicencio that had left that scent. It was Grandpa Vicencio making the smell of clay! The man cried and he laughed. She kissed the statue respectfully and was filled with a palpable longing for clay. Her hands worked an imaginary mass of earth. The sound of murmurs arose, of laments and laughter…Grandpa Vicencio. She listened carefully and took a deep breath. No, she hadn't lost contact with the dead. It was a sign that she would find her mother and brother among the living.

*P*onciá Vicencio's mother was always thinking about her children, but she dreaded the idea of setting out for the city. The city was for the young, for the ones that could still endure such rash adventure. Overnight the hair on her head had become white, but her face still retained a youthful appearance. Her heart weighed heavy inside her chest. It was as though she had a great clay pot within which she stored all of the people dear to her, and this receptacle had suddenly broken and shattered. She had suffered greatly with the departure of her daughter, and afterward, that of her son. Before that, she had born the weight of her husband's passing on that clear and shining afternoon. And she was accumulating these departures, passings, absences. There were moments when such desolation visited that she thought about quickening the hour. She felt so alone, so empty that she could go looking for clay over there, at the bottom of the river... Alone, but, somehow, recuperating. She believed that life had kept its own count, just like the fruit had its exact moment to be picked. She knew that her life was not yet a ripened fruit. Her days were not yet finished, it was not time for the harvest. And, therefore, if she had to suffer, she would feel the pain. If she had to be alone, alone she would be. If she had to feel the embrace of no one's arms but her own, she would create her own ring, and embrace herself, until she found her children and their embraces would wrap around the ones that she had created. .

Ponciá Vicencio ought to be very pretty. It had been such a long time that the daughter and son had left for the city and since then, she, too, had never stopped moving. When her daughter had gone, it had hurt. It was as though she had lost a part of her own body. The girl had transformed into a grown daughter. They talked, worked, and sang together. Even when she was very small, she had a special way with clay and knew how to go to the river and find it. She knew what kind was the best, what kind would be softer, what kind would do what she wanted. She recognized the kind that would congenially take orders from her hands, translating ideas into shapes for the sculptor. She knew the river's nature with her eyes closed. And whoever saw, just as she herself saw, when the girl began to go about with her closed-up hand curled behind, as if she had ended up with the cut off hand of the grandfather, would never believe that it was this very hand, a perfect mimicry of the old man's, that would give shape to the mass, that would be the greatest creator.

uandi José Vicencio wanted to be a soldier. He wanted to be Soldier Nestor. To be handsome like him in his uniform. To say just the right thing like he did. To speak with the voice of authority as he did. Soldier Nestor liked Luandi, enjoying the boy's openess. Sometimes he wanted to call him brother, but when he was around the other soldier, the white one, or the policeman, he restrained himself. He knew about Luandi's sister. He had asked around a bit to see if anyone had heard of a girl called Ponciá Vicencio, and he even went to the red light district to look for her. One day he took Luandi, but didn't tell him the real motive of their visit; a boy like him would be furious at the suggestion. They just went to look around for a date, and there were plenty to be found. Who knew, maybe one might be the boy's sister? So many of the girls that came from the country ended up there.

Soldier Nestor, when he could, when the police officer and the white soldier were on patrol and he was by himself, would teach Luandi how to sign his name. He felt for the boy; he liked him because he wanted so badly to become a soldier.

Luandi slept at the station. He had made it his home. One day he was seized by the urge to go back to his village. He checked with Soldier Nestor. Soldier Nestor asked the officer. It was settled. The boy had earned it. He worked hard. He was humble and eager. He could take some time off. Luandi kissed the hand of Soldier Nestor, but he still had one more request. Might Soldier Nestor have an old uniform that he could wear? He wanted to go back to his village like an important person, like someone in charge! Soldier Nestor didn't see any danger in it. Just as long as the other soldier, the white one, didn't hear anything about it, because then the officer would find out, too. Sure, an old, worn out uniform there in the closet. But he couldn't give him a gun or a club. He could go as a soldier, as long as he didn't mind going empty handed.

In the morning Luandi José Vicencio dressed up in the threadbare uniform that he had personally washed and ironed and, with his heart leaping in his chest, made his way to the station. The black boots, the ones that had been on his feet when he arrived in the city, were polished and shone like new. His boots pinched his feet, but he straightened his body and steadied his gait. A soldier does not limp; a soldier marches. He tried to make his body perform with the same elegance as Soldier Nestor's. He felt handsome like him. In the village everyone would be looking at him. The girls from his village, every last one, would want him for a boyfriend. His mother would be proud. He would go with her to the lands of the whites to show that he, a black man, now living in the city, could command, too.

On the nearly empty train, the few scattered passengers looked Luandi over from head to toe. He was thrilled. It made him feel important. He hadn't become a soldier yet – this was just a rehearsal – but the day would surely arrive when he would become a real soldier. The kind that makes arrests and pummels. The kind that goes to war. And there really could be a war... A war of blacks against whites? A war of rich against poor? No, not like that! He wanted to strike blows, make arrests... But if there really were to be a battle like that, what side would he be on? That was it! Only if it was a war of good against evil. There it was. He would be on the side of the just, and he'd give the evildoers a royal thrashing, and he'd put the wicked behind bars.

Luandi was so enthralled by these prospects – imagining the chance to command, to fight, to wage war – that when he came to his senses he was on his feet. He looked nervously around the train at his fellow passengers and saw that a young girl sitting in the back was smiling at him. He returned her smile without worrying further. The invention of a battle burned inside his mind. Suddenly, the thought was melted away by disappointment. Police station soldiers didn't go to war. Only the military soldiers did. Did they fight or not? Yes, they fight! No, they don't. He had to ask Soldier Nestor just as soon as he got back, as soon as possible!

*A*lthough she had not found her mother or brother, when Ponciá Vicencio returned from the village, she was filled with the certainty that they were both still alive. They would find each other – biding their time until the right moment for everything to unfold in order to become three again.

The hand continued to itch and bleed between the fingers. When this happened, she would be flooded with an immense nostalgia for the feel of clay. There had also been two or three times when the void that had filled her head came to visit. If she were standing at the sink or wash tub, it would take her by force, and she would have to wait for the feeling to pass. Sometimes it would take a while to go away. She was afraid that her mistress would see. She felt good about her job there, and what was more, she got to see the man that worked in construction right next door.

When Ponciá Vicencio's children, all seven of them, were born and then died, the first losses had brought great suffering. Afterward, with the passing of time and with each pregnancy, each birth, she found herself wishing that the child would not survive. Was it worth it to bring a child into the world? She recalled the poverty of her childhood and the terrible hardships of the fields, and she feared giving her own children the same kind of life. Her father had worked so hard. Her mother had struggled to get by selling pottery, and even so, they scarcely managed to provide a grass thatched roof under which to shelter their poverty. And that was how it was for so many. Children were covered in tatters until they were grown and then went practically naked. And when the girls were a bit older, the mothers would have to find a way to provide enough cloth to cover their sex and breasts. They would grow in poverty. Parents, grandparents, and great grandparents working always in the lands of the masters. Sugar cane, coffee, farming, ranching, land, all of it belonging to someone else – to the whites. The blacks were masters of misery, hunger, suffering, suicidal revolts. A few got out of the fields, ran to the city, their lives nearly bursting with misery, and hearts with nothing in them but empty hopes. She, too, had come to the city with a heart that believed in possibility, and where had that got her? A shack on the hill. Running about constantly to tend the mistress' homes. Some secondhand clothes and food scraps provided as compensation for the salary that was never enough. A despondent man, tired, maybe even more tired than she, and the despair when no other way to live could be found. It was good that the children had died. To be born, to grow, to live–for what? In the hovel next door lived Sá Ita with her five children. The eldest was seven and never stopped coughing and ailing. The doctor said it was a lung infection. But she didn't want to take the child to the hospital. He was going to die anyway; it was better that he die with her nearby. In front lived Durvalina with her seven children. One day, in the middle of the night, the youngest one, four months old, cried and cried. The father, in a fit of rage, probably drunk, snatched up the baby and flung him through the window. In the next place over lived Zé Moreira who worked in a restaurant kitchen. Every day he brought extra food home from work. One day it would be a nice cut of meat or a can of oil; on another it would be a package of butter. His wife knew that he was taking a risk, but it seemed that things would show up just in time, and if she didn't need it, there was always a neighbor who did. The kitchen manager had grown suspicious and said something to the owner. One day, when Zé Moreira was leaving, they asked to see his bag. He didn't just have leftovers, he also had a can of oil and two packages of butter. Zé Moreira was taken to the police so that he would serve as an example to the other employees. That was what happened when an employee stole. It was for the best that their children had been still born, and were free from having to live that life. What was the point of all the suffering of the ones who stayed behind? What purpose had the courage of those who had chosen to run away served, living like slaves in hiding? What good had it done, all of Grandpa Vicencio's anguish? He, in the act of courage-cowardess, had rebelled and killed one of his own and had even tried to kill himself, too. What good was any of it? The slave's life still went on. Yes, she, too, was a slave. Slave to a condition that kept repeating itself. Slave to despair, the absence of hope, the impossibility of launching new battles, organizing new communities, imagining a better life.

$\mathcal{O}$n her travels, in each place that she stayed, Maria Vicencio found pottery that had been crafted by her or her daughter. Time passed, life went on, and she, always busy, had never noticed how much she had created. Only afterward, in the calm she found away from her duties, could she reflect on what she had made. In every house, on every ranch, the pottery she and her daughter had made lived on. She easily recognized which were Ponciá's and which were her own. She had the impression that her daughter did not work alone, that some mysterious force guided the girl's hands. To go from place to place was a way in which Ponciá's mother alleviated the anguish of waiting and time. It nourished the certainty that she would find her children again some day, so she could not stop. She had to keep searching. The moments spent waiting in mute silence were worse; they made the wait even longer. On her pilgrimages, she worked at any job she could find – with the exception of making pottery. She never again put her hands to clay, but she continued to sing a lot, like in the days in which they had intoned songs together. She sang the old songs of her childhood, the ones she had learned from the elders from the time she was a little girl. She sang what she had learned from her mother and that she, in turn, taught her own daughter. Many of these songs were call and response, and when it came to the place in which her daughter's voice would come in, Panciá's mother was silent. She became quiet in order to hear a little girl's voice stir deep inside of her that, even though she had grown, even though she was far away, came forth to sing in her memories.

*S*leep finally got the better of Luandi on his journey home. He had only managed to remain alert for the first few hours. Anything could happen on the train (although nothing but railroad problems ever arose). If some mischief, a fight, or a mugging arose. he would be there to keep the peace. He would break it up like a soldier, with the voice of authority. The train traveled slowly, lazily, with no desire whatsoever to arrive. And, after a little while, as the afternoon gave way to night, the sleepy soldier grew slack in his efforts to maintain the order that was always being threatened. The soft shaking of the lazy train finally dulled his vigil. Evening grew into late night, and only afterward, long after early morning had ripened into day, did the disappointed Luandi awaken, already close to Vicencio Village. He had practically slept through the entire journey. He clumsily wiped away a string of spit that ran down his chin. He stole a furtive glance at the back of the train to look for the girl that had smiled his way. He saw that she was no longer there. She must have gotten off at some station along the way.

Luandi's feet throbbed inside the tight boots. He had to walk a long distance to get to his house. He would pass ranches, the lands of the whites, cross the lands of the blacks, and still have to overcome more terrain before arriving at the village. A hot sun seemed intent on melting the earth. As soon as he was off the train he took a few steps, sat down on the ground and, in an instinctive, furious impulse, flung off his boots. His toes that had been squeezed, massacred one on top of the other, were happy at the chance spread themselves. The soldier, now barefoot, drew a breath of deep relief. One step at a time, he began to cut into the distance that lay before him. Those who passed greeted him with a few words, raising a hand to their hat. Some asked after his mother and sister, saying it had been a long time since they had seen the two. Luandi began to feel stirrings of dread. They should be asking about Ponciá, but not about his mother. She had remained behind when he left, might have done some coming and going at times, but had to be there, on the land. What happened – was she gone? She wasn't selling, trading or giving away her work? She had been alone so long! He was also troubled by the fact that no one had noticed his soldier's dress; no one told him what an important man he had become.

Luandi took long strides to reach his home. It was an immense pleasure to feel his feet against the earth. He now walked in his own way, abandoning Soldier Nestor's gait. He felt a great heat beat down on his pretend soldier's clothing. He desired, with a burning passion, to be at the river where his mother and sister collected clay. That was where he had sumerged his naked body in the deep night of the forest, to bathe with his girlfriend and harvest his very first pleasure, inspite of the doubts surrounding his manly abilities.

Someone had recently cut back the growth, because in the rainy season it grew and surrounded the house of their mother, Ponciá Vicencio and Luandi. There were also traces outside of recently turned earth, as though someone were preparing to plant a small field. Luandi smiled. Their mother must be very strong to still be turning the earth. He sang out one of the songs that he had learned from his father from the days they had worked in the lands of the whites. It was a song that the eldest would teach the young. They said that it was the song of homecoming, in far away Africa, and would chant it when they returned from fishing, hunting or traveling in distant lands. When he wanted to charm his wife, Luandi's father would sing that song as he neared the house. Luandi didn't understand the words, but he knew that it was a language still spoken by some of their people, especially the elders. It was a happy song. Luandi accompanied his song with a rhythm made from clapping his palms against an imaginary drum. He was back on their land. He was home again. He sang and danced the sweet victory dance of homecoming.

The last sounds of Luandi's song flowed into space, but his mother had not appeared in the door as she had always done. The boy felt a tightening in his chest. Was it empty? How, if right outside there were signs of life? He pushed open the door that stood slightly ajar. Yes, their mother would definitely have to be there, at the river, perhaps…

Little by little, his mother's absence became a reality in Luandi's eyes and in his heart. Not a single ash lingered in the cold hearth. A snake had left its skin there to dry. The coffee strainer was dry and rotting from lack of use, confirming the absence of the living. His mother's clay cup remained intact, as well as the ones belonging to his sister and even his father. Where were they? He remembered his father and Grandpa Vicencio. He knew that both were present. Of his dead he knew, of the dead he understood and felt their absence-presence at all times. The worst was the absence of the living. He looked in the corner of the room, the side opposite the hearth, and saw the old trunk. He dragged the wooden stool over to it. Slowly and respectfully he opened the storage place where Ponciá Vicencio's memory of the old man was kept. He knew that his mother stored the clay man within. He also knew that his sister, when she had set out for the city in such a hurry that it seemed she was running away, had left Grandpa Vicencio behind. He felt around at the trunk's bottom, stirring its deepest memories. A shock came over him. The clay man had disappeared.

Luandi slowly recovered from his fright and felt a spreading joy take its place. No one would remove the clay man but Ponciá Vicencio. Not even their mother. Since the day in which their mother had shown their father the sculpture that the girl had made, and he had calmly and indifferently returned his daughter's work to her, from that day on, only Ponciá, its author, touched Grandpa Vicencio. It was she who, from time to time, would take up the clay man in her hands and spend long hours gazing at him. If the souvenir of the grandfather was not there, it was because his sister had returned to recover what she had left behind. Who knew, perhaps she had taken her mother with her? But as he scrutinized the appearance of the house, he noticed that there was no sign of a leave taking. Their mother couldn't be far, the door had been ajar. And he knew, then, that one day his mother and sister would return.

Surveying every inch of the house, Luandi saw from a distance the other room where his mother and father had slept. He had never crossed the threshold of that door. If he needed one of the two, he had always called from outside. When their father died, his sister began to sleep there in the bed with their mother, and that part of the house continued to be unknown to him. He remembered the conversations he had shared with his father. He would tell him that women were like stars. They were beautiful; they illuminated the night that lived in the hearts of men. They lived in other lands, had different ways, different dreams.

The memory of the two grew vivid and sharp inside of him. He looked once more at the room in which they had slept. He waited for a few moments, believing that they might still come out. When this did not happen, he headed for the exit, pushed the door open, and left. He could hear the voices of his mother and Ponciá, who always called out their blessing when it was time for him to go back to the lands of the whites.

$\mathcal{P}$onciá Vicencio didn't want to have anything more to do with the life that was unfolding before her. She was always seeing into other places and times. It didn't matter to her if the sun was out or if it was raining. Who was she? She couldn't say. She would happily anticipate these moments of self-absence. Before, she had enjoyed reading. She had kept several magazines and old newspapers. She would read and reread everything. There had been a time when she had learned the news by heart:

"*Child Dies of Asphyxiation in Latrine*"
Jair dos Santos, a young boy of three and a half, fell into a latrine that was located in the back of his home in the Wet Rat district. He was pulled out in critical condition by a team of firemen from the local precinct, and died at Saint John's Pediatric Hospital.

"*Bricklayer Kills Wife with Fifteen Stabs*"
Antonio Goncalves, bricklayer, became jealous after his wife had a conversation with a neighbor, returned home inebriated, and thrust his

knife into her fifteen times in the presence of their two children of five and three years of age. The victim died at the scene of the crime.

"Wife of Police Officer Arrested for Indecency"
The wife of Officer Joaquim Santana, Mrs. Neide Santana, was arrested when she was discovered with her husband's fellow officer, Officer Marco Brilhantes, while the two, stark naked, exchanged affections in the vehicle of Santana in Aroeiras Park.

"Misallocation of Funds in City Hall"
Mayor Antonio Pires opened an administrative inquiry to explain the misallocation of funds designated for the improvement of twenty public schools. The guilty parties, according to a deposition issued by the mayor, in which he promises to impose harsh penalties, will be exonerated upon the completion of public service, and will be asked to return the money with interest to the public coffers. The principal suspects are Mayor Antonio Pires' two closest advisors, his son Armando Pires and his brother-in-law Deocledio Tavares.

One day, Ponciá gathered all of the magazines and newspapers and used them to make a great bonfire. What difference did it make that she had learned to read? When she lived in the country, she had believed that in the city, reading would fling open at least half the doors in the world to her, if not all of them. Now she was no longer interested in any of the news: the policeman could just choke in the latrine, his wife could stab the mayor in the back thirty times, the boy could misallocate funds in City Hall, the bricklayer could hang around naked in the car and exchange all the affections he liked with that other officer. The world could just fall on its face, it made no difference because she didn't care, she didn't care...

Ponciá spent each day remembering life. That, too, was a way to live. At times, there was a remembrance made from such painful, such bitter memories that tears ran down her face; other times they were so sweet, so pleasant that her lips sprang into smiles and laughter. Her mother and brother were always the substance of her memory. It had been so long now. When would the three find themselves together again? Wanting to see them was her life. As such, nothing was done that did not involve waiting there calmly, seated in her corner, all but inert. It was necessary to wait. And that was precisely what she had been doing for years. She performed the functions that her strength permitted. And waiting was what it permitted.

$\mathcal{L}$uandi made his way quickly on the road back without knowing why. It wouldn't speed anything up if he ran. He would have to wait some fifteen days for the train, anyway. He would spend the days in the village. He could even go to Colonel Vicencio's ranch to see his companions from the fields and, who knew, maybe hear some news about his mother and sister. He was hungry and didn't have anything to eat. He had a little money, but in the lands of the blacks, food wasn't sold. Whoever was hungry just needed to go to someone's home and ask for it. And whoever had it would share their meal and refuse any money that might be offered in return. There was an enormous pleasure in offering, in sharing food with one another. And he could sleep just about anywhere, everyone would provide a traveler with a place to sleep, as long as their guest did not mind the poverty of the host. And so that was how he awaited his return to the city. By visiting with his friends from the fields, he discovered that his mother was alive.

A small handful had seen her, and heard her say that she missed her children dearly.

It was also during this waiting time when Luandi went to visit Nengua Kainda and ask for her blessing. The woman was as old as time, she looked like a mirage. Only her eyes conveyed the unspoken strength of her being. The sound from her mouth was nearly inaudible; meanwhile, her penetrating gaze absorbed everything and everybody around her. Nengua Kainda, speaking the language that only the eldest understood, blessed Luandi. She said that the boy's mother was alive and that they would find each other one day. She spoke of Ponciá Vicencio as well. His sister was in the city, not far from him. He needed to find her most urgently, to protect her before the inheritance was claimed. Afterward Nengua Kainda looked at Luandi's clothing and a laugh sprang from her eyes. Chuckling, she told him that he was on a path that was not his own. That he wanted to have the voice of authority, but what good was it to give orders if he was alone? If Luandi's voice was not to become an echo lending strength to the voices of his suffering sisters, not even in the desert would his language fall. Yes, it could even ensnare him, become sand in his eyes, a whip that he would lift against the bodies of his own relations.

Luandi did not understand her laugh, the mockery, the words of old Nengua Kainda. He had always listened to her, not only he, but everyone else from the village, as well. No matter – Kainda forgive him – with her blessing or without it, he was very certain that he would become a soldier some day.

After the fifteen days had passed, Luandi set out on the

train for the city. His heart was less afflicted, even though he had yet to discover not only the whereabouts of his sister, but of his mother as well. He had gone back to Nengua Kainda, and, even though he had not felt like seeing her again and was afraid of hearing new warnings from the old woman, he had entrusted her with his address. Unbeknownst to Soldier Nestor, he was with Luandi at all times. He went to give the woman one of the bits of paper that Soldier Nestor had put in Luandi's bag each time that he had sent the boy out to run an errand around the city, afraid that he might lose his way. Luandi had dozens of them, and had saved each one. Soldier Nestor had beautiful script. He would need to learn to read and write, too, one day.

On the return, he looked for the young girl that, on the first trip, had smiled at him on the train. When night fell, an insistent star made its presence known in the sky. He recalled again his father's words. Women were like stars. They were lovely. They enchanted the night that lived in the hearts of men

$\mathcal{P}$onciá Vicencio's husband began to think that his wife had taken ill. It was impossible to be so slow, so inane at the tasks that she had previously taken on with such vigor. It was true that when they had first met, she would sometimes be like that, going still. It seemed that she ran away from herself, but when she returned, it was as though nothing had happened. Not now. The absences, aside from being more frequent, left Ponciá outside of herself for longer periods of time. She spent hour after hour in the window watching the day go by with a blank stare. There was a time when he would hit, slap, yell... Sometimes she would get up and make their food, other times she wouldn't. There had been that day when he arrived tired, his throat burning for a drop of rum, but without a cent to his name to make this smallest of dreams come true. When he saw Ponciá frozen still, far beyond the living or dead, far from everything, he had to make her feel the aching too, and then he struck. He hit her, kicked her, pulled her hair. She didn't make

96

a single gesture in her own defense. When he saw the blood flowing from her mouth and nostrils, he thought about killing her, but the thought frightened him. He filled a cup of water from the pot and repentantly and affectionately cleared off his wife's face. She didn't react, she didn't show the slightest flicker of sorrow or rage. And from that day on, she was all but mute. She spoke only through gestures or glances. And she became more and more absent. He got up early and would find her sitting on the stool looking at the changing sky through the window. He made the coffee, packed his own lunch tin, and left a little food for her. Ponciá would just take a tiny mouthful of nothing, consuming only water. She would stare at him, but he could read little from her face. Neither hatred nor affection. must be possessed.

$\mathcal{L}$uandi contemplated the sky on his return journey with his eyes fixed on the stars – they seemed to be telling the train where to go, and he thought with longing about a particular star he had met. He really liked her, but couldn't find the courage to say this to anyone, not even Soldier Nestor. He had met her on one of the walks that the two would take on Saturday evenings along the strip where the women worked. Bilisa, like his sister, had come from the country, but not from his town. She had come to find work. She worked hard, saved a sum of money with the idea of going back home to get her parents and siblings. One day, no one knows how, her little box of money that she kept in the back of her wardrobe disappeared. Her savings were gone, the sacrifice of years and years. Bilisa was beside herself. No one entered that room except, on occasion, the son of her madam. Yes, he was the only one that came in, now and then, when he slept with her. He was the only one that could have taken the money – as a joke – probably to try to scare her. Her boss didn't like the suspicion that fell on her son. As for sleeping with a worker, that was fine. The madam herself had told the husband to encourage the game in order for the son to maximize their investment. The youth had dated a certain girl steadily since childhood, was going to get married soon, and Bilisa was such a clean and tempting employee. Bilisa couldn't find the money and never again saw the son of her madam.

The young Bilisa was aware of her fire, had slept a few times with her friends in the country and a few had become more and more passionate about their meetings. One day, in a fit of jealousy, one of them called Bilisa a whore. It didn't bother her. Whore just means someone who likes pleasure. That's me. Whore means hiding in the bushes with whoever I want? That's me. Am I a whore because I don't open my legs for someone if I don't want to? Then so be it. And now she was being called a whore again by the madam, just because she talked about the son sleeping with her. But she had been so sure that the madam knew. No, what she didn't like was hearing about the money. Bilisa was tired. She had to start over again from nothing. No, she wouldn't do it! The kitchen, the house cleaning, the cistern, the clothes iron… She had to get money faster.

When Luandi met Bilisa, she had already been working some five years or so on the strip and hadn't managed to save any money. She made a lot and was popular, but she spent a lot, too. The money was handed back to the landlady and Black Climerio, their protection. There were also certain occasions when she wouldn't be paid. If the man that sought her had given her pleasure, had made her forget for a few moments that her job was to provide pleasure for the other, or if she sympathized with him, if she liked him for any reason, Bilisa didn't charge. She thought that feeling good did not have a price. And that was how she began to be the star that enchanted the night that existed in Luandi's heart. It was after an encounter of sweet pleasures, in which the two, naked, even before touching each other, for no reason or motive, had begun to tell each other about their lives. When they looked around, the day had already passed them by outside. They had been talking for hours and hours. And the rest of the clients? Soldier Nestor must have already finished with his lady and left by then. When Luandi pulled the bill that was already folded inside his pocket and handed to the girl, she refused to accept it. She said she liked him so much and that feeling did not have a price. He was quiet when he left, but bursting with joy. He strolled for a while, delaying his departure from the district. Soldier Nestor was gone. It frightened him a little. It was the first time that he had found himself alone on the strip. He quickened his pace out of the district. At the end of the block he bumped into Black Climerio. It startled him. But Black Climerio hadn't even noticed Luandi. He was caught up in a tune that he whistled into the night.

$\mathcal{L}$uandi had not abandoned the dream of one day becoming a soldier. He came back from the land troubled by Nengua Kinda's words, but, even as he made his clumsy entrance at the station and saw Soldier Nestor, he decided to forget the words from that conversation, the laughter and mockery of the old woman. He would really do it, and what was more, he had to do it in order to be able to find his mother and his sister, to have the power to arrest Black Climerio and take Bilisa out of the district so that she would enchant the dark night that he carried in his heart.

Luandi wanted to have a conversation with Soldier Nestor. He wanted to tell him that he was falling for Bilisa. After all, he was a close friend. He was even teaching him how to read. Would Soldier Nestor say something? Could it be that he might disapprove because Bilisa was a working girl?

Soldier Nestor did not like Luandi's choice. He said that the boy had lost his mind. According to Soldier Nestor, working girls were no good. They weren't able to care for just one man. What was more, come to think of it, working girls didn't like any man. They only liked what a man had between his legs and, even then, only when it came with money. And since he didn't have any money, she would be sick of him right away.

Luandi let Soldier Nestor speak. He thanked God, though, when his friend, finally changing the subject, sent him to find his pencil and notebook for the day's lesson. Luandi was learning to spell his name. He already knew how to write Luandi José; only Vicencio was left.

What a shame! Soldier Nestor didn't like Bilisa at all. He was very wise, understood so many things, had pretty writing, was well spoken, too, but in this particular matter he was completely ignorant. He didn't know that working girls had feelings, too. Bilisa herself, from the time of their first encounter, had refused to take his money. If Soldier Nestor did not know, did not understand, did not believe, then it was not he, Luandi, who would try to file this new fact in his friend's head. He spoke no further of Bilisa. He decided to let time go by. And one day, when he had become a real soldier, he would take Bilisa from the district, marry her and make children, and then Soldier Nestor would become Godfather Nestor. It was just a matter of time. Luandi was happy. His life felt lighter. In the dark night that inhabited his heart, there was a guiding light, a woman-star called Bilisa.

*I*n the month following the boy's return from his land, a robbery was reported at the station where Luandi José Vicencio worked. Not far from there, in the salon of a club, there was an exhibit of popular art. A few pieces had been stolen. The police officer went along with Soldier Nestor. Soldier Nestor liked the displays that he saw very much. The pieces were all made from clay, bringing back memories of his days in the fields (Soldier Nestor was also from the country) and of Luandi. The boy would definitely love this exhibit. He would bring the boy with him later so that he could appreciate all of these works. And, on his day off, Soldier Nestor planned a surprise for Luandi. Instead of taking the route to the red light district, the path they traveled every weekend, he set out in the direction of the club. Only when they approached did he tell Luandi what they were doing there. And when Luandi heard that they were going to an exhibit of clay works, the nostalgia for his mother and sister that lived inside his chest pulled so suddenly and violently that his eyes moistened with tears. He hastened to wipe them away with a quick and clumsy gesture, afraid that his friend might notice.

Luandi saw life in the fields blossom in his memory as he contemplated the objects of his past before him. He saw his mother and sister making house wares and decorations from the thick mass of earth. He was enchanted by a family of birds. The mother bird, the baby chicks, and the father bird. He liked the scene's simple harmony. He asked his friend to read the card that accompanied the pieces. Soldier Nestor read:

Artist: Unknown
Region: Municipality Engenho Cruzado
Owner: Colonel José Maria da Cruz

With his eyes drunk from everything he saw, Luandi was at once lost and rediscovered in the midst of the displays. He stopped for a long time to look at each object, until, regretfully, he would move on to the next table. That was when, to the surprise of Soldier Nestor, he lovingly took up a little clay cup and in a strangled voice, almost a sob, cried: "It's mine! It's mine!" And, as a child might, he stroked the piece, calling out to his mother and to Ponciá, not heeding the urgent whispers of Soldier Nestor, who took the piece back in an attempt to return it to the display. And, without Luandi having to ask it of him, his friend, greatly moved, took the little white placard that was beside the objects and read:

Artists: Maria Vicencio and daughter Ponciá Vicencio
Region: Vicencio Village
Owner: Dr. Aristeu Pena Forte Soares Vicencio

Luandi looked at the pieces made by his mother and sister as though for the first time, recognizing himself in each one of them. He observed the minutiae of each piece. There were the utility objects: pans, pots, pitchers, cups, and then there were those for decoration, smaller, tiny. People, animals, miniature house wares, all fantasy pieces, enchanting things, play things, creations made as though the two of them wanted to miniaturize life so that it might endure forever, fitting anyplace, every place, in the eyes of its keeper.

And, not able to contain the tears any longer, Luandi took the little white placard and made out the names of each of them, wanted to take the inscription with him, but replaced it instead. It gladdened him to see that his mother and sisters' creations were accompanied by the names of the authors. On the previous table there had been such a lovely work of art and the name of its creator went unknown. With his family, this was not the case. What he did not recognize was the name of the owner. Who was he? There also had been so many white family members and masters populating his countryside. All were land owners. Some to a greater, others to a lesser extent, but they always owned something there, in the village or beyond. He did not capture the fact that that was precisely who Vicencio was.

*M*aria Vicencio knew that, for all her reluctance, one day the city would also be included on her mission. She did not have the slightest desire for the adventure of the journey. If her life was the land, that on which she lived, then what would she do when she found herself away from it? Even so, she prepared herself to withdraw from the land of her birth. The land guarded her buried umbilicus, sealing her connection to the soil of her people. In the womb of the earth, vestiges of their own wombs had also been placed. Maria Vicencio had repeated this same ancient and protective gesture with her own children, just as her mother had done with her.

And, like one fulfilling the preparatory rites for the undertaking of an important journey, the mother of Ponciá and Luandi began to take leave of her home. With each departure, she returned, and when she left again, she increased the distance from the starting point, advancing a little further on her course to find her children. The ritual of coming and going had been completed several times. On the first return she had not found any signs of them at all, but when she came back a second time, she reaped news of her daughter. Nengua Kainda spoke of her. And when she returned for the third time, Old Nengua spoke of her son and gave her the address that Luandi José Vicencio had left. She believed, then, that she was prepared, thought that the time had arrived for her to go and seek her children, but was warned that time had not yet ordained a reunion for the three.

Maria Vicencio heard the words of Nengua Kainda and agreed. Why go against time, the Elder advised in her whisper of a voice that was made from silences more than from sounds. Humans do not have the power to abbreviate time, and when they insist on it, they harvest green fruits before they are ripe. Everything has its given time. Didn't she see the seeds? The people plant and it is necessary to forget about the life hidden beneath the soil until, one day, at the exact moment, independent of the desire of the one who strew the seeds, it breaks through the earth, sprouting life. Nothing better than ripened fruit, picked and eaten at the precise moment, the right way. Her reunion with her children also belonged to time's march and not just her own. Her desire was the pact she made with life. It was a tract to be watered with patience; the faith that the best was yet to come. Yet again, Maria Vicencio returned to her home, still pregnant with her children, waiting for the day in which she, mother, would be reborn.

$\mathscr{P}$onciá Vicencio's husband nudged her softly on the shoulder and beckoned with a cup of coffee. A delicious fragrance permeated the air. She looked at him with a start, murmuring that she would get up. He stopped her, touching her lightly on the face. A tremor of fear traveled through her. Would he strike again? She squeezed her eyes shut and braced her body to await the blows. He, with clumsy affection, tried to lift her face, which caused her to curl inward even further. He regretted that he had hit his wife so many times. No, she was not distant or dull out of laziness. She was sick, very sick. A strong spell that someone had cast. His eyes wandered over to the lunch tin above the hearth rolled up in newspaper that he needed to take with him to work. He set the cup down on the windowsill, making a little sound in the hope that Ponciá might understand it was for her. Nothing. Worried, he did not know what to do. Ponciá rarely ate. He would come home late from work, always to find her sitting on the stool in the same place

108

by the window, looking out. At times she was calm, her look was distant, almost gay; other times she was irritated as though caught in a web of bitter visions. It was time to go, but he didn't want to leave Ponciá Vicencio that way, coiled up in fear. He stood waiting for a little while. He took down the coffee tin and held it close to her nose. Another shudder went through her, and only when she had deeply absorbed the smell of coffee did she timidly lift her face to look into his. She took the cup and moved it to her lips, finally recognizing her husband's intentions.

On the day Ponciá's husband had beaten her to the point in which blood had poured freely from her mouth, he began to recognize the suffering that he had inflicted on her. He never struck her again, and instead began to treat her with affection. It was so great the fear, the suffering, the pain that he had read in her eyes when he cleaned away her blood, that he saw in them not only her homelessness, but his own as well. He discovered that they were alone. He saw that each guarded their own mysteries. He felt that, even though they had been living together for years and years, they were like strangers to each other. He discovered that, although they had met so many times to exchange pleasures of the flesh, even though she had housed his seed inside of her and this seed had been transformed into life seven times, through it all, they were both desperately alone. From that time on, after witnessing the solitude of his mate and that of himself, he began to regard her as a fellow creature, and was infused with a great tenderness toward her. That was when he began to understand her utterances. The emptiness that she

109

said she felt where her dead father and grandfather belonged; her missing mother and brother. At times, she would also say that she missed the feel of clay, and from time to time, an itching would emanate from between her fingers that she scratched until they bled. Ponciá Vicencio's husband, since he was not to have a different kind of life with his wife, came to terms with what he did not understand. And, even when he felt the need for pleasure fill his sex, he left her alone, seeing that it had been a long time since she had abdicated all urges of this kind. Little by little, more and more, Ponciá went deeper into a world that was hers alone, in which he, there on the other side, as much as he cared for her, could only stand on his side of the impenetrable door.

$\mathcal{T}$he longing that Luandi José Vicencio felt for his mother and sister grew with each passing day. He felt guilty about his inability to locate them. Neither the success he was having with his writing nor the company of Bilisa managed to assuage the heaviness in his chest. He wanted to go back to the village, but was afraid that he wouldn't find any news and he dreaded the thought of having to listen to more of old Nengua Kainda's words.

Soldier Nestor noticed the boy's sadness. He began to think that he was unhappy with his work. Luandi explained the reason for his heavy heart. Soldier Nestor listened and understood, knew from his own experience what it meant to be alone; he, too, lived far from his people..

Late that afternoon, one in which the sorrow would not loosen its hold on Luandi, he finally gave up on the magazine that he had been half-heartedly leafing through, paying no attention to its words. Inside of him, in the dark night that filled his heart, shined the image of Bilisa, who brought with her moments of peace and awakened his thirst for living. This consolation brought him to his feet, and he set out for the district. If there was a dark night in his heart, what better than to find the star that enchanted his life. Bilisa was that guiding light. How he wanted that lady! Lady Bilisa, lady-star, lady-life... Oh! He was discouraged needlessly, loosing faith just when things were getting close to changing for the better. This very year he would become a soldier. He was going to earn more money and become somebody. He was nearing the point in which he could buy a little home and get Bilisa out of the district. She wanted to go with him. She loved him, and what was more, she was sick of being exploited by Black Climerio and her life in the district. Bilisa was his now. And Black Climerio knew it. He gave Luandi hard looks, but he didn't dare meet him head-on, knowing full well that the boy worked at the police station. Soldier Nestor had told Luandi that he would become a soldier before the year was out. The officer was handling the whole process. The forms were on their way, it was just a matter of reading them and signing. The possibility of seeing this dream come true worked to dissipate a little of his suffering. He was close – soon he would be wearing an important uniform. It was what he wanted most of all. His mother and sister, when he found them, would certainly approve. Nengua Kainda was a wise woman whose words rang true, but, in his case, Nengua had been wrong. There was nothing more to it; he was to become a great soldier.

Soldier Nestor still didn't like Bilisa. He often told Luandi that he was wasting his time, that any second she would give him a kick in the ass, just as soon as someone came along with an open fly and bigger wallet. Luandi listened, but never replied. His friend really had it in for working girls. But Bilisa was not a working girl; for him, Bilisa was simply woman-star.

Luandi had already told Bilisa that, as soon as he became a soldier, he would get a house, and, if she wanted, she could come to live with him. She wouldn't have to work anymore, and they would have lots of children. The day he told her that he wanted to take her with him – if she chose – the girl didn't give any sort of answer or sign of consent. But when he returned the following week, there was a surprise. She began to open several packages: there were bolts of cloth to make sheets, towels, bedclothes, everything they needed. Spools of brightly colored thread, needles, trimmings. She wanted to have everything ready; she said she wanted to make a pretty wedding dress in the time between her visits from the men who came to see her. But, in the midst of so much happiness, Bilisa-star revealed an apprehension. There was a conflict that she did not know how to resolve. Black Climerio. The man was a threat.

When Luandi noticed, he was just arriving at the strip where the women worked. He had already been there so many times before. Such a long time had passed since he had first come to the city, years that he had spent hoping to better his life, but it had been worth it. It had cost him dearly, he had struggled and suffered. He had learned to read; could write his own name and was going to learn so much more. Soldier Nestor had been father, God, brother, friend. And to complete his happiness, he had found the right star, all his own: Bilisa, the guiding star to illuminate each night of his life.

From the corner, Luandi could see up to the floor where Bilisa lived. It was a big house, old, with many rooms. Fights were constantly breaking out amongst its many visitors and inhabitants. One day, a fire broke out. Some of the women had run naked and screaming into the street, but that had been the worst consequence of the incident. Other members of the household managed to put out the flames with buckets and cans of water. Luandi had been on her floor that day. He was so occupied with Bilisa-star that, when he finally noticed it, the flames had already been doused.

As he neared the house, Luandi met Black Climerio. When he saw him, the man lowered his head and quickened his pace as though he wished to run. From up in the house someone gestured frantically for Luandi to come while, from Bilisa's window, others pointed at him and at Black Climerio. Luandi couldn't make it out, but sensed that something was happening. He looked around; Black Climerio had already disappeared. He must have been running to be able to get around the corner that fast. Luandi ran in the opposite direction, quickly reaching the door of the house. In a second he was in Bilisa's room. And that second was the last he had to take her into his arms and see his Bilisa-star, covered in blood, flickering out.

Black Climerio had killed her. On the bed were the yards of cloth, the spools of thread, and the needle she had used to prepare her gown. Luandi trembled. Black Climerio had killed his Bilisa-star. He killed her! He killed his wife! He killed the

114

woman who was going to be so happy. No, it wasn't true! Black Climerio was always such a bum. Bilisa had warned him, but he could not believe that a man that cowardly had it in him to attack her. The night that he carried in his heart became a starless black.

Luandi José Vicencio was shaken from the nightmare by someone touching him on the shoulder. He raised his eyes that were still mired down by the image of the dead woman, and saw Soldier Nestor, his brother, his friend. Soldier Nestor gave Luandi an embrace in the midst of the gathering crowd, whispering into his ear that he had been arrested. Luandi, dumbstruck, asked him who. His friend regarded the other's grief with compassion, and explained in a stronger voice that they had arrested Climerio. It seemed as though his friend didn't care. His only concern was for the moment in which his Bilisa-star had gone out.

$\mathcal{M}$aria Vicencio raked the ashes on the hearth once more to see if the cinders were lit. They all were, but one incandescent ember stood out from the rest as brightly as a star. Three days had passed since the mother of Ponciá Vicencio had returned to her home. Since the children had gone, she had always lived there, but she was unable to stay still. She returned to visit the home, scatter the emptiness and feel the presence of the dead. On more than one occasion she had discovered the empty skin of a snake, and she would cut away the foliage outside. When she cleared the growth, she was also driving away her doubts about venturing into the city. She had to take the train and find her children to bring them back to the land. She had waited patiently for several years. She had suffered much, it was true, but had learned in the process that it was impossible to go before the time was right. On this particular homecoming she had visited Nengua Kainda. The woman was lying on the mat in the terreiro, resting calmly with her eyes closed. Ponciá and Luandi's mother stood for a moment, taking in the other's weariness. She was very old. It seemed that in her, the years of all the elders on earth put together were congregated. Overwhelming sorrow swept over Maria Vicencio – she thought that the woman was dead. Nengua Kainda then made a light, vague movement with her hand, ordering Maria Vicencio to lower herself down. She obeyed. The old woman opened her eyes to seek those of Maria and, once more, was able to see into her life and into the life that awaited her. The voice, diluted by time, sounded almost like a dream, a whisper, but Maria Vicencio was able to make out what the old Nengua Kainda was saying. She told her that time was ready to open the doors that would lead her to her children. And with these last words, with the force from behind her closed eyes, eyes that now saw even more penetratingly, Nengua blessed the voyage that Maria Vicencio would undertake to be reunited with her children. Ponciá and Luandi's mother waited for the elder to form another gesture or request. At that moment, for a brief instant, the whole world seemed to stand still. Nengua Kainda had gone to sleep. A hot sun beat against her black skin, wrinkled with the contours of centuries. In silence, she entered a deep sleep from which she would only awaken when she had traversed the limits of another age, another space, manifesting even older, ever wiser, in another epoch.

*W*hen the train, after an interminable string of days and nights, finally pulled into the station, Maria Vicencio painfully stretched her legs. Throughout the journey she had been curled around the bundle that she held tightly to her breast, bent deeply in prayer. Her bladder was heavy and she needed to relieve herself, but fear would not permit her to get up and use the train's facility or the ones to be found along the way when the machine halted. As soon as the train stopped, the younger ones that had spent the entire trip wandering from car to car scampered out. Through the train's window, her eyes scanned the crowd. No one. The first thing was to get rid of the fear. She was terrified of the city, but knew with certainty that she would find her children there. She did not know how to read, but she knew how to speak. She descended, taking a few first steps intoxicated by a courage that she had conjured up out of sheer will. Searching, she spied a black soldier in the far corner of the station. Excited, earnest strides carried her in his direction. His heart gave a joyful leap without knowing the

118

reason for the sensation that, in all its years of service, this was the moment for which it had been waiting. It was not the fist time he had experienced such a thing. There were passengers that, when they came to the city, it was as though they walked right into his heart. When Luandi José Vicencio arrived, he had already been waiting for him. It had not been his day to go to the train station at all, but the other soldier, the white one, had taken ill. And when the mother of Ponciá and Luandi handed Soldier Nestor a small, folded up piece of paper, nearly worn through by time, that she had painstakingly folded into a piece of cloth and placed between her breasts, he smiled to recognize his own handwriting. It was as though he had known all along. He had been the one to pen the address that Luandi had left that day with Nengua Kainda so that the elder could, in turn, deliver it to his mother. Maria Vicencio liked the young soldier who looked close enough in age to Luandi to have been her own son.

Soldier Nestor took the woman's bundle, gently wrapped his arm around her shoulders, and headed in the direction of the police station. He was joyful. It was as though she were his own mother that he had not seen for many long years. And, like a son that, upon reuniting with his mother, was reawakened to his own true self, he imagined the happiness with which Luandi would awaken.

When Soldier Nestor arrived with Maria Vicencio at the station, her chest could scarcely contain the heart within that felt like it would explode with anticipation. My God, so much time! What would the boy be like? She remembered him small, serious, polite, the very image of his father. She would find Ponciá Vicencio next, and the three would return home. Luandi had steady work in the city – would he leave it behind and go back to work in the fields? What if he wanted to become a soldier like his friend?

Soldier Nestor, after handing the woman a glass of water sweetened with sugar, afraid that the joy of seeing her son might very well be too much for her, went to find Luandi. He found the boy seated at the edge of his bed with his face in his hands. After Bilisa's death, the boy never left his room for any reason other than to fulfill his duties around the station. Lately, he was nourished only by the taste of suffering. He wept often. When Bilisa-star had been put out, the absence of his mother and sister weighed on him even more heavily. A few days later, after the event, the officer had summoned him. With Soldier Nestor at his side, the officer had told him that the case had truly been a shocking one, even for him. Never in all his years of service had he investigated such a brutal crime. He told the boy that he would have to recuperate; would have to learn that not every woman was going to bring him happiness. When Luandi went to the district – after all, he was a man, and a bachelor, at that – he would have to do as Soldier Nestor. Get in, sow his oats, and come back ready and able. None of this falling for working girls. He should consider himself lucky; Black Climerio could have done the same thing to him. And Luandi mustn't take what he was going to say the wrong way, but most blacks were vagabonds, vandals, and thieves who were up to no good. Few, only a very few, were like Soldier Nestor or like him. Soldier Nestor shot an uneasy glance at Luandi, who remained clam, placid, distant, as though the officer were not making himself heard at all. His only thoughts were for Bilisa-star, the light that had been so violently put out in his life. So, on the day when Maria Vicencio appeared before Soldier Nestor and he, enraptured, had playfully called Luandi over to see who had been arrested, Luandi's heart dislodged the pain that deafened his ears. The taste of blood came into his mouth. His only thought was that he had brought him Black Climerio. But hadn't his friend already said, on the day it happened, that they had arrested him? The other had been forced to take hold of Luandi by the arm and all but drag him out of there. Again he retreated gratefully into his solitude, without feeling remotely interested. It was from within this state that his eyes fell upon his mother, and he was overcome by a sudden rush of emotions and images. Luandi could not discern if it was a dream or a newly unearthed reality that he met. His mother, Ponciá, Bilisa-star, the woman who so recently enchanted the night that lived inside his heart, Grandmother Vicencia, a person he had never known and whose death had been met at the hands of Grandpa Vicencio. And there were even more women that he had never seen and of whom they had seldom spoken. These women approached him at that moment. And, among them, the one that oriented the footsteps of the rest. The one who acted as guide to the rest, the old Nengua Kainda. It was she who had led Maria Vicencio to him. Awakening from the lull of mixed dreamstate and vigil, Luandi was finally able to comprehend that his mother had arrived. When? How had she come? Did Soldier Nestor know? And his sister Ponciá, what had become of her? No, she didn't know, either, the girl had disappeared...

Luandi's mother touched Luandi's life like a healing light. Her presence helped the son endure the pain of Bilisa-star's death. Downcast, he did all he could so that it would escape her notice, but some mothers have eyes like a hawk. Maria Vicencio felt each tear that Luandi would only allow to flow on the inside.

And then, a small happiness found its way into his life. The papers to become a soldier had finally arrived. Soldier Nestor, the white soldier and the officer all congratulated Luandi, and his mother gave him a tearful embrace. He had become a soldier. He was happy. Now it was just a matter of taking the money he had saved over the course of several years to buy the little home that he had dreamed of getting for Bilisa-star and himself. It was urgent to find a place in order to take care of his mother and later, together, in which to bring Ponciá Vicencio. His mother spoke with such certainty about finding her daughter that she managed to put him at ease. Any day now, his sister was going to turn up.

$\mathcal{P}$onciá Vicencio grew more and more disturbed. She would get up from the stool where she had been sitting so often over the last several years by the window and begin to pace in tight circles within the confines of their small house. She spoke to herself often, now crying, now laughing. She begged for clay, she wanted to go back to the river.

Ponciá Vicencio's husband went to work with a new worry burdening his beleaguered frame. He feared that he would come home and find that the woman was missing. The neighbors told him to shut her away in a hospital. He didn't want to, but many times he found himself admitting in his mind that she truly was very ill. He intuited, however, that Ponciá Vicencio just needed to live out her mysteries, fulfill her destiny.

One day, after looking through him as though he were not there, after so many years of withdrawal, buried half living, half dead inside the house, Ponciá Vicencio smiled, chortled, cried, saying that she knew what it was that had to be done. She would take the train, go back to the village, go back to the river. Saying this, she took the clay man out from underneath the stool. She arranged a few pieces of cloth, and with a gesture summoned from her earliest days, one that recalled her mother's custom, asked aloud if there weren't a few banana leaves and corn husks to be found with which to wrap the figure. She promptly made a small bundle and slowly withdrew from their home.

The bewildered man followed Ponciá with his face lowered to conceal himself. What was she going to do? He knew that if he tried to stop her it would be worse. He would go with her, he would follow her to see if he could bring her back, knowing fully well that for a long time now she had been going, going, going... Ponciá Vicencio walked downhill. She headed in the direction of the river.

*A*part from their headquarters, the first place in which Luandi would render service was the train station. He was thrilled when the officer told him. He would experience the place in a different way. He wasn't someone that was simply arriving. He was someone who had arrived. He was a person who had gotten somewhere. The uniform that he wore smelled fresh and new, and his feet were shod in boots. His feet, whose toes were now capable of taking orders, had been tamed by his previous shoes and were now broken in. He fit his weapon to his belt, regarding himself in the mirror. Not bad. He remembered Nengua Kainda. His mother told him that the elder had passed. A slight shudder traveled through him. Even so, he took firm strides – practically marched – into the new life that he was about to inaugurate.

Calm pervaded the station. No arrivals or departures were scheduled. Luandi smiled proudly at the custodian that cleaned the station. A new black soldier, a railroad worker observed. He

125

didn't know this one. He only knew Soldier Nestor. He wanted to go up to Luandi and wish the brother well.

Now that his greatest wish had been realized, Luandi wanted to believe that his future would be one full of granted wishes, in spite of the image of the star that had gone out in the dark night of his heart. He was a soldier. He had the power to command. Everything would be easier, even finding his sister. Uniformed, donning his costume of of authority, he could go anywhere and have everyone's respect – respected by all. And whoever had any news of Ponciá Vicencio, yes, whoever knew of her whereabouts, they would just have to speak right up. Mesmerized by these thoughts, in the sway of future orders that he planned to give, enjoying the preview of the pleasure he would derive from his commands being heard and obeyed, Luandi's eyes combed the area under his control. There had to be something around that needed his attention, his say. He had to exercise his new authority. How – wasn't anything going to happen? His eyes wandered from one side of the station to the other and discovered, out of the blue, the figure of a woman who came and went, pacing aimlessly, almost in circles, on the far side of the station. And even though the station was small, Luandi perceived a distance of centuries rise up between himself and the woman-mirage. A silhouette from afar that was infinitely slow in concretizing itself before his gaze. And, finding that he could not take a step in the desired direction, his voice compelled itself to cry out a name.

Ponciá Vicencio's name echoed through the station like the whistle of the train and she paid not the slightest attention to its call. She paced, cried and laughed, saying that she wanted to go back to the river. Luandi gently approached his sister, telling her that he knew the way to the river so he ought to take her. Ponciá Vicencio looked at him, but whether she recognized him or not was impossible to say. At that moment she unfastened her bundle to withdraw the clay man and asked her brother if he remembered Grandpa Vicencio. He, who until now had been choking back a sob with terrific effort, let the tears flow as he took his sister into his arms.

He abandoned his post on his first day of active duty before the end of his shift. He took his sister's hand and the two set out to join their mother. The time had come, and Maria Vicencio was growing anxious. She couldn't wait any longer: the moment had arrived to find her daughter and return her to the river.

$\mathcal{P}$onciá Vicencio's husband kept himself from the others in silence. Through closed eyes, their mother saw a web of images: the girl, Grandpa Vicencio, his passing, the passing of her husband, the wisdom of Nengua Kainda, the lands of the blacks, the works in clay, the son who had now become a soldier, the voice of authority, the lands of the whites, the frightened resistance – often so silent – of her people veiled by a superficial obedience to the whites. Time flowing back and forth. And in its goings and comings, Ponciá Vicencio was returning to her. No, not to her! The girl had never belonged to her. She was going back to the river, to the mother-waters. The girl had never fit inside her, not even when she had been pregnant. Maria Vicencio remembered the first sign that the girl was not her own. She had always kept it to herself; it was a silent thing. She didn't even tell her husband, only Nengua Kainda, the one who knew all, even the things that no one told. The news that the girl was growing in a borrowed womb had come when she had been seven months along. One morning, Maria Vicencio awoke to the sound of a child's crying. She strained to listen. When she tried to find the source of the sound, she was shocked. The crying came from inside of her. The child cried from inside her womb. She stroked her belly to comfort the child that was incubating until it was time to be born, feeling the movements of her kicks and sobs. What should she do? What should she do? How could she alleviate the cry of her offspring still inside of her, so mournful that it seemed it to know the infinite suffering of the world? Her intuition led her to the river, and as soon as she stepped into its waters, the sounds of pain that her daughter made grew calm. Ponciá Vicencio cried three days straight from inside her mother's womb. Four moons later, she was born with a tiny, yet deep cackle that issued from the newborn's throat. Ponciá never learned of the tears she had spilled into the waters of her mother's placenta. Maria Vicencio was always careful to keep it a secret for the girl's sake; a person that cried in their mother's womb should never find out about it.

Maria Vicencio, now with her eyes opened wide, contemplated her daughter. The girl was still beautiful; her suffering face wore the features of a grown woman. For a few moments, other faces – not only that of Grandpa Vicencio – visited Ponciá's countenance. Her mother knew them all, even the ones that arrived from another space and time. There was her daughter one-and-many. Maria Vicencio was glad, the time to conduct her daughter home again, to the river's edge, was ripening. Ponciá would go back to the place of the waters where her life force, her sustenance, lived.

uandi José Vicencio looked into his sister's worried face as she paced in circles. She was so very pretty. Ever since she was a little girl she had such ability with clay, had so much talent for sculpting raw earth in her hands. One day he would go back to the land and try to gather some works that she and his mother had made. Pieces that would tell part of a larger story – the history of his people. His sister had the gestures and manners of Grandpa Vicencio. It wasn't a surprise that the similarity grew with each passing day. She had finally been made the vessel, the heir to a history of all their suffering, and while this suffering lived on in their memory, those that embodied it would not be able to forge a new destiny, not even by force. And he, who had so wanted to become a soldier, to give orders, to fight, to make arrests, all of the sudden discovered that fulfilling this dream was worse than useless, as it would never lend meaning to his life. Soldier Nestor was as weak and subservient as he was. All he did was follow orders, even when he gave them to others, even when he made arrests. It was imperative that Grandpa Vicencio's inheritance be fulfilled, be realized in his sister for him to understand it in its entirety. Only now did the laughter and words of Nengua Kainda become clear to him. He, who had spent so much time longing to become a soldier, in a few brief minutes abandoned that life. Soldier Nestor, his brother, would not understand. How could he possibly explain what he had just then figured out? In the same way that he had believed that being a soldier was the only way to be, he had now made a new discovery. He had understood that his life, a grain of sand at the bottom of the riverbed, would only take shape and grow if it was connected to the lives of others. He realized that it was not enough to read and sign his name. Reading had to open out onto a greater knowledge. He had to become the author of his own life, just as he needed to help construct the lives of his relations. And he had to continue to decipher in the vestiges of time the meaning that had been left behind, and to understand that, within the signature that flowed from his hand, resided other letters and markings. Life was an amalgam of before-now-after-beyond. Life was a fabric made from everyone and everything. The ones that went before, the ones that were now, and the ones that would come to be.

Ponciá Vicencio, she that had cried from inside her mother's womb and cackled newborn laughs at her birth, had laughter on her lips, even when the whole of her body trembled with a cry of pain and confusion. She cried, laughed, muttered. She unraveled the twisted strings of a long history. She paced in circles, now with one hand shut and curled around her back, as though it were cut off, now with palms held open, executing calm and rhythmic movements, as though shaping a mass of live matter. Ponciá Vicencio was painstaking in her imaginary act of creating. Zealous in her art, she took care of the extra portions, the excess mass, just as she would have cared for the amputations and absences that formed part of the body. Her hands kept on and on with their inventing. And when the molding of art was interrupted, it was as though the alternate gesture was a molding of life, attempting to fuse the pieces together in a single act, melding both sides of the coin. Her steps marking the wheel began to quicken, without disengaging the work of her hands. She walked as though to reconcile one time with another, kept taking hold of it all, the past-present-still-to-come.

And of the time recalled and forgotten of Ponciá Vicencio, one image presented itself from the sheer weight of its existence: Grandpa Vicencio. From the parapet of the little window, the figure of clay twisted to look partly outside, partly inside, crying, laughing, seeing it all.

There outside, in the iris-hued sky, an enormous, multicolored angorô cascaded slowly down, while Ponciá Vicencio, link and heir to a memory newly uncovered by her relations, would never be lost; would be kept in the waters of the river.

Conceição Evaristo was born in Belo Horizante in the state of Minas Gerais. She is a professor of Brazilian literature at the Catholic University in Rio de Janeiro (PUR/RJ) and is working on her doctorate in comparative literature. Her work deals with the social factors influencing the family, including the power that women exert in their role as mothers and the consequences of society's failure to provide adequately for its youth. Her work has been published in the following anthologies: various issues of *Cadernos Negros; Vozes de Mulheres* (1991); *Schwartze Prose; prosa negra-Afrobrasilianische Erzählungen der Gergenwart* (1993); *Moving Beyond Boundaries. International Dimension of Black Women Writing* (1995); *Finally Us. Contemporary Black Brazilian Women Writers* (1995); *Callaloo*, vol. 18 number 4 (1995).

Paloma Martinez-Cruz, PhD, is Assistant Professor of Latin American Literature at North Central College in Illinois. Originally from California, she received her PhD from Columbia University in New York. Her areas of specialization include U.S. Latino writing and performance, Mexican fiction, and Brazilian literature, film, and popular culture. She has translated criticism and creative writing from both Spanish and Portuguese into English, and has given professional and creative presentations in all three languages in the U.S., Mexico, and Brazil. Paloma endeavors to include hemispheric perspectives in her teaching and research, publishing and presenting on topics such as shamanism and globalization, East Los Angeles lowriders, Brazilian cordel literature, Cinema Novo, and hemispheric questions of gender and colonization.